Cogwheels
and Other Stories

Cogwheels
and Other Stories

Ryūnosuke Akutagawa

Translated by Howard Norman
Illustrated by Naoko Matsubara

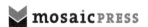

Library and Archives Canada Cataloguing in Publication

Akutagawa, Ryūnosuke, 1892-1927
[Selections. English]
    Cogwheels and other stories / Akutagawa Ryūnosuke.

Issued in print and electronic formats.
ISBN 978-1-77161-067-4 (pbk.).--ISBN 978-1-77161-068-1 (html).--
ISBN 978-1-77161-069-8 (pdf)

    I. Norman, Howard, 1905-1987, translator II. Title.

PL801.K8A2 2014   895.63'44   C2014-906159-5
                                                C2014-906160-9

Pubished by Mosaic Press, Oakville, Ontario, Canada, 2015.
Distributed in the United States by Bookmasters (www.bookmasters.com).
Distributed in the U.K. by Gazelle Book Services
(www.gazellebookservices.co.uk).

MOSAIC PRESS, Publishers
Translations Copyright © 1982, 2015, Howard Normann
Illustrations Copyright © 1982, 2015, Naoko Matsubara

Printed and Bound in Canada.
ISBN Paperback 978-1-77161-067-4
         ePub 978-1-77161-068-1
         ePDF 978-1-77161-069-8

Design and layout by Eric Normann

Mosaic Press recognizes the support of the Ontario media
Development Corporation, OMDC, for our publshing efforts.

We acknowledge the financial support of the Government of Canada through the Canada Book Fund (CBF) for this project.

Nous reconnaissons l'aide financière du gouvernement du Canada par l'entremise du Fonds du livre du Canada (FLC) pour ce projet.

Canadian Heritage   Patrimoine canadien

Canadä

MOSAIC PRESS
1252 Speers Road, Units 1 & 2
Oakville, Ontario L6L 5N9
phone: (905) 825-2130

info@mosaic-press.com

www.mosaic-press.com

Contents

Ryūnosuke Akutagawa

RYŪNOSUKE AKUTAGAWA was born in Tokyo in 1892. His mother went insane eight months after his birth, and died ten years later. He was given over to the care of his mother's older brother, Akutagawa Michiaki and his wife. Akutagawa's father went bankrupt, and later he too went insane. As a child, Akutagawa was puny and sickly, and suffered from poor health all his life.

Physically he was a wreck, intellectually he was brilliant. He passed into the First Higher School in Tokyo by recommendation without having to write entrance examinations and then entered Tokyo Imperial University, the number one Japanese university. He graduated with honours in English Literature in 1916. His graduation dissertation was entitled "A Study of William Morris."

Even before graduation he had achieved literary distinction. "Rashomon" was published in the magazine *Shinshicho* in 1915. The popular film of the same name, directed by Kurosawa Akira, was based on two of Akutagawa's tales: "Rashomon," and "In a Grove."

Akutagawa was widely read in Chinese, Japanese and European literatures. He drew on various sources for his stories and many of the one hundred and fifty stories he wrote derive from classical tales, which Akutagawa reinterpreted in the light of modern psychological insight. It is very likely that Akutagawa wrote the story of Kandata in "The Spider's Thread," for example, after reading Grushenka's "fairy tale" in *The Brothers Karamazov*.

Shortly after he wrote "Cogwheels" in 1927, Akutagawa committed suicide by taking an overdose of sleeping pills.

The Akutagawa Prize, established in his honour several years later, is the most coveted literary prize in Japan and has attained much the same prestige as the Prix Goncourt in France.

Naoko Matsubara

BORN AND brought up in Kyoto, Japan, she studied at Kyoto Academy under Viennese artist Frau Lizzi Ueno. She received her M.F.A. from Carnegie Institute of Technology in Pittsburgh and also stayed at the Royal College of Art in London as an invited student.

Naoko Matsubara has exhibited widely in North America, Europe and Japan. Her work is to be found in many of the major galleries and museums of the world: the Albertina, Vienna; British Museum, London; Museum of Fine Arts, Boston; Cincinnati Museum of Art; Fogg Museum, Harvard; Haifa Museum, Israel; Klingspor Museum, Germany; National Museum of Modern Art, Tokyo and Kyoto; Philadelphia Museum of Art; Smithsonian Institute, Washington, D.C.; and, the White House, Washington, D.C.

She now lives in Ontario, Canada. Her books include *The Tale of the Shining Princess* (Kodansha International, Tokyo, 1966), *Boston Impressions* (Barre Publishers, Barre, Mass., 1970), *Solitude,* a series of 11 woodcuts in Portfolio, based on a chapter from Henry Thoreau's *Walden* (Aquarius Press, N.Y., 1971), *Kyoto Woodcuts* (Kodansha International, Tokyo, New York, San Francisco, 1978) and *In Praise of Trees* (Mosaic Press, Oakville, 1984).

Howard Norman

HOWARD NORMAN was born in Karuizawa, Japan in 1905. His parents were Canadian missionaries in Japan, and Rev. Norman has spent most of his life in Japan as a missionary with the United Church of Canada.

From 1941 to 1947 Rev. Norman was minister of St. George Church in Vancouver. He spent the next twenty-five years in Japan, first at Kansei Gakuin University, and later in Shiojiri, Nagano Prefecture.

Rev. Norman first became interested in Akutagawa's literature after reading Glenn Shaw's translations. Rev. Norman's translations of four Akutagawa stories were published in 1948 in Japan and have been reprinted in the United States.

Howard and his wife Gwen retired to Toronto where he passed away in 1987.

Acknowledgment

I WOULD like to express my special appreciation to Panasonic Canada whose support has realized this unique partnership between a Canadian publisher, a great Japanese writer, a distinguished Japanese artist, Panasonic Canada, and myself.

Howard Norman

Cogwheels

I HAD LEFT A SUMMER RESORT WITH ONE SUITCASE TO attend the wedding of an acquaintance. I was hurrying in a car for a certain station on the Tokaido.[1] Pine trees grew thickly on either side of the road. It was doubtful whether I would make my train for Tokyo. The only other passenger in the car was the proprietor of a barber shop, as fat and round as a jujube, with short whiskers. Though I was worried about the train, I exchanged a few words with him.

"Odd things happen, don't they," he said. "They say there's a ghost haunting X's big house, even in daylight."

'In daylight, eh."

"But apparently not on fine days. It appears most often, they say, when it's raining."

"It appears on rainy days to get a wetting."

"You're joking. But they do say this ghost wears a raincoat."

Tooting its horn, the car drew up at the station. I parted from the barber to discover that the train had left by a bare two or three minutes. In the waiting-room a man wearing a raincoat was sitting listlessly on a bench, looking out of the window. I thought of the ghost I had just heard of. Smiling sourly, I went into the café across from the station to wait for the next train.

Though it was called a café, this was only a courtesy title. I sat at a table in the corner and ordered a cup of cocoa. The oilcloth on the table was white, checkered with irregular blue lines; the thin canvas showed through dirty at the corners. I drank the stale cocoa and looked around the empty room. Paper signs with "Oyako donburi,"[2] "Cutlets" and so on were pasted on the dusty walls. "Fresh eggs." "Omelettes."

When I read these signs I was reminded that this was a country station on the Tokaido—a place where electric trains sped through wheat fields and cabbage fields.

It was almost sunset when I boarded the train. I always travelled second class, but this time, I don't know why I travelled third.

The train was crowded. All around me were public school girls who, it appeared, had been on an excursion to Oiso. I lit a cigarette and watched them. They were all very lively and kept up a constant chatter.

"Mr. Photographer (Shashinya San), what is a 'love-scene'?" The photographer who sat in front of me, had gone along with the excursion; he was having fun with the girls. A girl of fourteen or fifteen persistently asked questions. Suddenly I noticed that she had a sort of boil on her nose and could not help smiling. Then a girl of twelve or thirteen who had been standing beside me climbed on to the lap of a young woman teacher, put an arm around her neck and stroked her cheek with her other hand. She chatted with her schoolmates, but from time to time she would say to the teacher, "What a darling you are, sensei (teacher). What sweet eyes you have."

If you ignored the way they munched their un-peeled apples and peeled the wrappers from their car-amels, they were, I felt, grown-up women rather than schoolgirls. An older girl passing me must have stepped on someone's foot. Instead of saying "Sorry," she said "Gomen nasai" (I beg your pardon). But somehow she seemed to be more of a schoolgirl than the rest of them. I puffed at my cigarette; only I seemed to notice the dis-crepancy. I could not help smiling sourly to myself.

The lights in the carriage were turned on and the train reached a suburban station. I stepped on the plat-form in a cold wind, crossed the bridge and waited for the Metro. Then by chance I ran into T who works in a firm. While we waited for our train we chatted about the depression. Of course he knew more about its prob-lems than I did. He wore a turquoise ring; apparently the depression had not touched him.

"That's a fine ring you have."

"This? A friend who's been in business in Harbin had me buy it from him. He was in difficulties—couldn't do business in a cooperative."

Fortunately the train we boarded was not as crowded as the one I had just left. We sat down together and chat-ted of this and that. I had returned in the spring from a visit to Paris and we talked about Mme Caillaux, about lobster dishes and of the travel abroad of a certain prince.

"France isn't as badly off as you would expect, you know. But Frenchmen hate paying taxes, so they're al-ways changing cabinets."

"But the franc is badly devalued."

"That's according to the newspapers. But just go to France, my friend. According to the newspapers there's nothing in Japan but earthquakes and floods."

As he said this, a man in a raincoat entered the carriage and sat down in the seat opposite us. I felt uncanny and shuddered. I wanted to tell T the story of the ghost in X's house. But T twirled the handle of his cane to his left and looking straight ahead, said in a low voice:

"See that woman over there? With the mouse-colored shawl?"

"The one with her hair done Western style?"

"Yes, the woman with the furoshiki. She used to be very chic."

Anyone would have said that now she looked very shabby. Still chatting with T, I glanced cautiously at her. Something about her eyes made me feel she was a bit queer. A sponge that looked like a leopard skin protruding from her furoshiki[3] bundle.

"In Karuizawa she danced and went around with a young American. She was a modahn gahru."[4]

By the time T and I parted the man in the raincoat had disappeared. Bag in hand, I left the Metro and headed for a certain hotel. Both sides of the street were lined with high buildings. As I walked along I recalled the pine forest; suddenly a strange something appeared in my field of vision. A strange something! They were whirling, semi-transparent cogwheels. I had often seen them before. They kept increasing until they blocked my sight. It did not last long, but when the cogwheels faded out, I was left with a headache—it was always like this. My oculist had often warned me that because of my hallucination I should cut down my smoking. But I had seen the cogwheels at the age of twenty before smoking had become a habit.

It's starting again, I thought. In order to test my left eye I covered my right eye with my hand. There was nothing wrong with my left eye, but outside my right eyelid there were the cogwheels whirling around. The buildings to the right of me gradually seemed to fade away.

I checked my hat and coat and took a room. Then I phoned the office of a magazine to talk about money.

* * *

THE WEDDING banquet had been in progress some time when I sat down in a corner and picked up my knife and fork. The bride and groom at the front and the fifty-odd guests around the U-shaped table were, needless to say, very gay. But under the bright electric lights, I felt myself becoming more depressed. I began to talk to the guest beside me in order to drive away my gloom. He was an old gentleman with white-whiskered cheeks exactly like a lion and also, as it happened, a famous scholar of Chinese with whose name I was familiar. It was natural that our talk should soon turn to the classics.

"A Kirin (unicorn) is a one-horned animal. And a *ho-oh* is a phoenix." The famous classicist seemed to be interested in what I was saying. As our conversation proceeded, I began to speak in a forced way and was possessed by a neurotic desire to be iconoclastic. I suggested that Yao Shun was an imaginary person and that the author of Ch'un Ch'iu wrote much later than the Han dynasty. Whereupon the scholar became openly unpleasant. Without looking at me he interrupted me almost with the snarl of a tiger. "If Yao Shun did not exist then Confucius told falsehoods. A sage would not tell lies."

Of course I remained silent and applied my knife to the meat on my plate. As I did so, a maggot began to crawl quietly along the edge of the meat. It brought the English word "worm" to my mind ... There was no doubt that this word, like the unicorn and the phoenix, meant a certain legendary animal. I laid down my knife and fork and looked at the champagne which had been poured unobserved into my glass.

At last, when the banquet was over, I walked down a quite deserted hall in the hotel to the room which I had taken. It felt more like the hall of a prison than a hotel, but fortunately my headache had almost left me.

They had brought my hat, my overcoat and bag to the room. My overcoat hanging there on the wall seemed to be myself standing up. I hastily threw it into a corner of the closet.

I went to the mirror and stared steadily at my face. Reflected in the mirror, it revealed the lines of the bones under the skin. It promptly recalled the maggot on my meat-plate.

I left the room, opened the door and walked aimlessly down the hall. At the corner which led to the lobby there was a tall bridge-lamp with a green shade whose light was brightly reflected in the glass door. Somehow it gave me a sense of peace. I sat down in a chair in front of it and thought of various things. But I had not been sitting there five minutes before there was the raincoat again, thrown carelessly in the long chair at my side.

"A raincoat at the coldest time of winter." With this thought I once more walked back through the hall. There was no bellhop in the corner of the hall where they usually waited, but their voices came to my ears faintly. It was a reply in English. "All right ... *Aw raito.*" I fretted, trying to catch the course of the conversation. *"Aw raito. Aw raito."* What was all right?

Of course my room was quiet. But when I opened the door I felt uncanny as I entered. Hesitating a moment, I then walked in confidently and sat down at the table so that I could not see the mirror. The chair was an easy chair, covered with greenish, lizard-colored morocco. I opened my bag and took out some manuscript paper to continue with the short story I had been writing. But the pen I had dipped in the ink would not move. When it did, all it would write were the words: "All right ... All right ... All right, sir ... All right."

Suddenly the telephone by my bed rang. Startled, I leapt up and put the receiver to my ear.

"Who is it?"

"It's I. I ...." The speaker was my older sister's daughter.

"What is it? What's the matter?"

"Something dreadful has happened. Some ... Something dreadful has happened and I've just phoned Auntie." (The narrator's wife.)

"Something dreadful?"

"Yes. So please come at once. At once, do. you understand."

The phone went dead. I hung up and automatically pressed the bell button. I was sharply conscious that my hand was shaking. The bellhop was slow in coming. I was more distressed than irritated and pressed the button again and again. At last my destiny had taught me the meaning of those words "All right."

My sister's husband had that afternoon committed suicide by throwing himself in front of a train in the country not far from Tokyo. He had been wearing a raincoat, an odd time of year to wear one. I resumed work on the short story. It is midnight; no one walks along the hall. But occasionally outside my door I hear the sound of wings. Maybe somebody is keeping a bird.

II Vengeance

I WOKE in that hotel room about eight in the morning. But when I started to get out of bed, oddly, there was only one slipper. For a year or two this occurrence had always filled me with fear and anxiety. It reminded me of the Greek myth of the prince with only one sandal. I rang for the bellhop and asked him to look for the missing slipper. He looked at me strangely and searched the little room.

"Here it is, sir. In the bathroom."

"How did it get there."

"Maybe a rat."

When he left I drank black coffee and began to polish the short story. The square window panes, framed in volcanic rock, looked out on a garden covered with snow. In pauses between writing I glanced out idly. The snow under the budding daphne bushes was soiled with the sooty smoke of the city. It was a scene that for some reason distressed me. Smoking a cigarette, I stopped writing and began to think of various things. About my wife, my children, and also about my sister's husband.

Before he committed suicide he had been suspected of arson. Not surprising, for before setting fire to his house he had insured it for twice its value. By dint of perjuring himself, he had received a suspended sentence. I was uneasy not so much because he had committed suicide as because I had certainly seen his house burning when I had returned to Tokyo.

From the train I had either seen a fire burning on a mountain or from a motorcar (I was with my wife and children then). I had seen a fire in the vicinity of Tokiwa Bridge. Before his house had burned, he had himself given me a premonition about it.

"My house may burn down this year, you know."

"What an unlucky thing to … But it would be dreadful if it did. And it isn't properly insured."

That is the sort of thing we were saying. But my house had not burned. With an effort I drove out the phantasms and picked up my pen again. But try as I would, the pen would not write a line. At last I left the table, threw myself on the bed and began to read Tolstoi's "Polikouchka." The hero of this story is a complicated mixture of vanity, honour, and morbid tendencies. If his tragi-comic life were altered a little, it would be a caricature of my own. The feeling of the irony of destiny in this tragi-comedy gradually made me feel weird. Before an hour had passed I leaped from my bed and threw the book with all my might into a corner of the room where the window curtains hung. "To hell with you!" and a big rat ran out from under the curtain diagonally across the floor towards the bathroom. With one jump I was at the bathroom, opened the door and looked around for it. The rat was not under the bathtub. Suddenly I felt a shudder, in a panic changed from slippers into my shoes and went out into the deserted hall.

It was still as gloomy as a prison. With bent head I ascended and descended stairs until I found myself in the kitchen. It was surprisingly bright. The flames danced in the ranges flanking one wall. As I passed I was conscious of the cool stares of the cooks in their white caps. And all the time I felt again that I had fallen into hell. "May God punish me. Don't be angry, God, or I may die." I could not keep the prayer from rising unbidden to my lips.

I stepped out of the hotel and plodded off to my sister's. The blue sky was reflected in the snow melting in the streets. The leaves and branches of the trees that lined the streets were blackened. They were lined up, front and back, exactly like people. This aroused dread in me rather than a sense of weirdness. I recalled the souls in Dante's Inferno who had been transformed into trees, and turned to walk along a street with street-car tracks, lined with buildings. But even here I could not walk a hundred yards in peace.

"Pardon me for speaking to you like this."

It was a young man of twenty-two or three in a student uniform. I looked at him and said nothing. I noticed a mole on the side of his nose. Cap in hand, he addressed me timidly.

"It's Mr. A, isn't it?"

"Yes."

"I thought it was you."

"Did you want something?"

"I just wanted to meet you, sir. I am a great admirer of your works."

I raised my hat and walked away from him. "Sir ... Mr. A These expressions had recently become most uncanny to me. I believed that I had committed every conceivable sort of crime. And they were still calling me "Sensei," teacher, when opportunity offered. I could not help feeling that something was sneering at me. Something? But my materialism was denial of any mystical beliefs. Only two or three months before I had published the following in a friend's magazine:

"I have no conscience, and in particular, no aesthetic conscience. All I have is nerves."

My sister had taken refuge with her three children in a shack at the end of an alley. Inside the shack, which was papered on the outside with coarse brown paper, it seemed colder than outside. With our hands on the edge of the brazier we talked of this and that. My sister's husband, a man of sturdy physique, had instinctively despised me—a thin, scrawny person. Not only that: he openly declared my work was immoral ... For my part, I had always looked down on him; never once had I had a good talk with him. But as I chatted with my sister, I gradually became aware that he, like me, had fallen into hell. It was as though he actually saw a ghost in the sleeping car. I lit a cigarette and deliberately talked only of money.

"Since it's come to this, you'll sell everything, I suppose."

"Of course. How much will the typewriter fetch?"

"Yes. And there are the pictures."

"Will you sell N's (my brother-in-law's) portrait? But that ..."

As I looked at the unframed conte[5] I felt I could not joke about it lightly. He had been run over by a train, his face a bloody pulp with only his moustache remaining. The affair was most unpleasant.

The portrait was perfectly drawn with the exception of the moustache which was sketched vaguely. I thought it might be the way the sunlight fell on it and looked at it from a different angle.

"What are you doing?"

"Oh nothing. Simply that in that picture, around the mouth ..."

My sister glanced at it and answered as though she had noticed nothing amiss. "His moustache does seem a bit odd, a bit thin, isn't it."

What I saw was not an illusion. But if there was an illusion[6] ... I prepared to leave so that I would not put them to the trouble of giving me lunch.

"What's your hurry?"

"Tomorrow, maybe. I have to go to Aoyama today."

"Oh, there. Are you unwell again?"

"Yes, I take drugs all the time. The sleeping pills alone are something. Veronal, neuronal, trional, numal."

Thirty minutes later I entered a building and took the elevator to the third floor. I tried to open the door of a restaurant there but it was closed. A lacquered sign with the word "Closed" was hanging on it. I was annoyed, for I could see apples and bananas piled in dishes on the tables. I returned to the street. As I did so, two men who appeared to be in business, talking animatedly, brushed by me as they entered the building. It sounded as one of them said, " ...irritated, you know." I stood on the street and waited for a taxi. Not many were passing, but those that did were all painted yellow. (Those yellow taxis seemed to me to be involved in traffic accidents.) Then I saw a green taxi lucky green and started off for the mental hospital near Aoyama Cemetery.[7]

"Irritated ... tantalizing ... Tantalus ... Inferno."

I, Tantalus, saw the fruit through the glass door. Twice I cursed. Dante's hell came floating into my eyes and I stared hard at the taxi-driver's back. Again I began to feel that absolutely everything was a lie: politics, business, art, science—all without exception were nothing else to me than enamel which concealed this frightful life. I breathed more and more painfully and opened the taxi window. But the sense of something strangling my heart did not leave me.

My taxi reached Meiji Shrine street-car stop. The sidestreet which led to the hospital should have been there. But today for some reason I could not find it. After having the taxi drive me up and down the street several times I gave up and got out.

I found the sidestreet with some trouble and turned in onto its muddy surface. I lost my way and came out at the Aoyama funeral hall. I had not been near it since Natsume Soseki's funeral which had been held there ten years ago. I had not been happy then either, but at least I had been at peace. I looked at the gravel-strewn walk under the gate and recalled the banana plant in "Soseki Sanbo" (the name of Soseki's study). I felt that something had brought me to the cemetery in the tenth year since the funeral.

I left the hospital and rode a cab back to the hotel. When I stepped out at the entrance, a man in a raincoat was quarrelling with the bellhop. A bellhop? No, not a bellhop but the commissionaire in a green uniform. I felt it would be unlucky to enter the hotel and promptly turned back into the street.

It was almost sunset when I came out on the Ginza. I could not help feeling more depressed than ever at the shops on both sides and the bustling people who crowded the sidewalks. It was particularly depressing to see all the people walking along as if they didn't know such a thing as sin.

I walked on and on in the fading daylight that was blending with the electric lights. Then my eye was caught by a bookshop that was piled high with magazines and books. I entered and browsing along the bookshelves, picked out a volume entitled "Greek Myths." The book, bound in yellow, had apparently been written for children. One line I happened to read struck me like a blow. "Even the greatest god, Zeus, is no match for the god of vengeance."

I turned my back on the bookshop and walked back into the crowd, unable to forget that god of vengeance.

III Night

ON THE second floor at Maruzen's[8] I found Strindberg's "Legends" and glanced at two or three pages. What was written there did not differ much from my experiences. And—the book was bound in yellow. I returned it to the shelf and pulled out a volume at random. One of its illustrations showed only cogwheels with human eyes and noses. (It was a collection by a German of drawings made by lunatics.) Gradually I felt resistance rising within me against the depression in which I had been sunk. Like an inveterate gambler who is bankrupt I opened book after book after book. But in each volume in sentence or illustration there was something to needle me. In every book? Every time I had read Madame Bovary—and I had read it often—I could not help feeling I was that middle-class man, M. Bovary.

Dusk had fallen. Apparently I was the only customer on the second floor of Maruzen's. I wandered through the bookshelves under the electric lights. I stopped in front of a shelf labelled "Religion." ... In the table of contents of one book there was one chapter entitled: "Four Dreadful Enemies: Doubt: Fear: Pride:

Carnal Desire." I felt my resistance mounting. These enemies, so far as I was concerned, were only sensitivity and intellect under different names. It was intolerable that the traditional spirit as well as the modern spirit should make me miserable.

With the book in my hand I suddenly remembered "The Young Man of Shou Lin." "Shou Lin" was the pen name I had once used. This was a story of a young man in the Han Fei Tzu collection who before he had learned to walk in the manner of Kantan, had forgotten how to walk like a man of Shou Lin, and returned to his native place.[9] Today there was no doubt that in the eyes of everybody I was that young man of Shou Lin. But I had used this pen name before I had fallen into hell—I turned my back on the bookshelf and with the effort of one trying to banish illusions I walked into a room opposite where there was a display of posters. But there, on one of the posters was a knight like St. George killing a winged dragon. The sullen face of this knight under his helmet partly revealed a face that resembled one of my enemies. Again I remembered the story of the skill of the dragon-killer in the Han Fei Tzu collection, and without passing through the room where the posters were displayed, walked down the wide staircase.

Night had fallen. I proceeded along Nihonbashi and continued to think of the word "dragon-killer."[10] This was certainly the name inscribed on my ink-stone. A young man had given it to me. After having failed in various enterprises he had at length become bankrupt a year ago. I looked up at the sky and thought of how small this globe would be in the light of those countless stars—and therefore, how small I was. However the sky that had been quite clear during the day was now quite clouded over.

Suddenly I felt something hostile to me and took refuge in a café on the other side of the streetcar tracks.

I was certainly taking refuge. I felt peaceful, however, in the rose-coloured walls of the café and sat down comfortably at the farthest table. Fortunately there were only two or three customers. Drinking a cup of cocoa, I smoked my usual cigarette. The blue smoke rose faint against the rose walls. The blend of these two gentle colours pleased me. But after a little I noticed a picture of Napoleon on the wall to my right and again I gradually began to feel uneasy. When Napoleon was a student he had written at the end of a geography text, "St. Helena, a little island." We would say this happened by chance. This much, however, was certain—it terrified Napoleon.

Staring at Napoleon, I thought of my writing. The first thing to drift into my memory were the aphorisms from the "Sayings of a Midget"—in particular—"Life is more hellish than hell itself," then of the fate of Yoshihide, the hero of "Hell Screen." Then, blowing out the smoke of my cigarette, I stared at the centre of the café in order to escape these memories. I had taken refuge here only a few minutes ago, but the appearance of the café had changed completely. What made me particularly uneasy were the imitation mahogany chairs and tables which did not harmonize with the rose-coloured walls. Again fearing that I would be overcome by suffering invisible to human eyes, I threw down a silver coin and started to leave the café.

"Wait a minute; twenty sen please."

What I had left was a copper coin.

Smarting under the humiliation, I walked alone down the street. Suddenly I recalled my house in the distant pine grove, not the house of my adoptive parents but the house I had rented for my own family. I had lived in it for about ten years. But because of certain circumstances I had moved to live with parents. At the same time I had become a slave, a tyrant, a feckless egotist.

It was about ten by the time I returned to the hotel. Exhausted by my long walk I had not even the strength to go up to my room, but sank into a chair before the big logs in the fireplace. There I thought of the long work I had been planning. This was a series of more than thirty short stories starting with the period of the Empress Suiko,"[11] and proceeding to the Meiji Era in stages. The hero in each case would be the people of the periods, as I watched the sparks dancing up, I suddenly thought of the bronze statue in front of the Imperial palace.[12] This statue, in helmet and armour, like the very spirit of loyalty towering high, bestrode his horse. But those who were his enemies—it's a lie.

I slide back from the distant past to the immediate present. Then by good luck, one of my seniors, a sculptor, appeared. As usual he was clad in velvet and sported a goatee. I stood up and grasped his outstretched hand. (This was not my custom, but he had lived half his life in Paris and Berlin—it was his habit.) His hand was strangely slimy, like a reptile's.

"Are you staying here?"

"Yes."

"Working?'

"Yes, working and …"

He stared fixedly at my face, eyeing me, I felt like a detective.

"Won't you come to my room for a chat," I said to him defiantly. (This defiant attitude in a nature lacking in courage was one of my bad habits.)

"Where," he asked with a smile, "Is your room?"

Shoulder to shoulder like old friends, we made our way through some foreigners who were talking quietly, to my room. When we reached it he sat down with his back to the mirror. We talked about various things? But mostly about women. There was no doubt about it—I was a man who had fallen into hell because of the sins I had committed. That only and the talk of vices at length depressed me. For a time I became a puritan and scorned those women.

"Look at S's lips. Because they have kissed so many ..."

Suddenly I shut my mouth and stared at his back reflected in the mirror; a piece of yellow sticking plaster was stuck on just below his ear.

"Because they have kissed so many?'

"Yes, I think she is that sort of person."

He nodded, smiling. I felt that he was inwardly watching me, unremittingly in order to learn my secrets. Yet our conversation did not leave the subject of women. Rather than hating him I was ashamed of my weakness and finally could not help becoming melancholy.

After he left, sprawled out on my bed I began to read *Anya Koro, (A Dark Night's Passing)*.[13] Each of the hero's spiritual struggles was painful to me. When I compared myself to him, I felt what a fool I had been and wept. But at the same time the tears brought peace to my feelings, but not for long. My right eye was beginning to see those semi-transparent cogwheels again. They were whirling around as usual and gradually multiplied. Fearing the onset of a headache, I left the book by my pillow, took eight grams of veronal and fell into a deep sleep.

In my dream I was staring at a pool. A crowd of boys and girls were plunging and swimming. I turned my back on the pool and walked towards a pine forest beyond it. Then from behind me someone called "Daddy." I looked back and discovered my wife standing in front of the pool. And as I did so I felt bitter remorse.

"Daddy, where's your towel?"

"I don't need a towel. You must look after the children."

Again I started to walk away. But what I was walking on had become a platform. It appeared to be a country station with a long platform bordered by a hedge. A university student and an old woman were standing there. When they saw me, they walked towards me and addressed me one after the other.

"What a big fire that was."

"I barely escaped."

I felt there was something familiar about the old woman; moreover I felt a pleasant excitement in talking to her. Throwing up a plume of smoke, a train drew quietly along the platform. Alone I boarded the train and walked along the berths on both sides; they were all curtained. On one of the berths, the nude body of a woman, almost a mummy, fading out, was lying. Undoubtedly it was my god of vengeance—some madwoman.

I opened my eyes and without thinking immediately leaped out of bed. The electric lights were still on. Somewhere was the noise of wings and of a rat squeaking. I opened the door and quickly went out into the hall to the fireplace where I had been before. I sat down in front of it and watched the flickering flames. A bellhop in a white uniform walked up to it to add some kindling.

"What time is it?"

"About half past three, sir."

In spite of the hour in the far corner of the lobby a woman who appeared to be an American was reading a book. Even at a distance it was apparent that she was wearing a green dress. I felt almost as though I had been saved and waited patiently for the dawn. As an old man who has passed through long years of painful illness waits for death.

IV Still Continuing

AT LAST I finished writing the short story in the hotel room and sent it to a certain magazine. The fee, of course, would not be enough for a week's stay, but I felt satisfied at having completed it and started out for a certain bookshop on the Ginza to get a spiritual tonic.

Scores of scraps of paper were scattered on the asphalt on which shone the wintry sun. Possibly the sunlight made them seem exactly like roses. I felt a sort of goodwill and entered the bookshop. This place also appeared more attractive than usual. But a little girl wearing glasses who was talking to a clerk bothered me a bit. Recalling the roses on the Street—scraps of paper—I bought *The Dialogues of Anatole France* and an edition of Merrimée's letters.

I entered a café with the two books and sat down at the farthest table to await my coffee. Opposite me sat a couple that looked like mother and son. Except that he was younger than I he resembled me almost perfectly. The couple were talking with their heads close together like two lovers. As I watched them I noticed that the son

was consoling his mother almost in a sexual way. This was certainly an instance of that affinity which I had known before—and at the same time of the will that makes hell of this world. Then just as I began to fear that I would be plunged again into suffering, fortunately my coffee arrived and I began to read Merrimée's letters. In these, as in his novels, his aphorisms scintillated. At one time his aphorisms had fortified my feelings like iron. (Over-susceptibility to this influence was one of my weaknesses.) Finishing my coffee, with a feeling of 'let come what may' I stepped briskly out of the café.

As I walked along the street I peered into several shopwindows. One picture-framer had a picture of Beethoven on display. His hair standing on end it was the exact likeness of a genius. I was absurdly moved by this Beethoven. Then suddenly I met an old friend, a friend of junior college days. Now a professor of applied chemistry, he was carrying a large folding suitcase; one of his eyes was quite bloodshot.

"What's the matter with your eye?'

"This? Just conjunctivitis."

I remembered that fourteen or fifteen years before whenever I had felt an affinity, my eyes became inflamed with conjunctivitis like this. But I said nothing. He clapped me on the shoulder and we talked of friends. Then still talking, he led me into a café. "It's been a long time. Not since the Shu Shun Sui memorial ceremony, I think,"[14] he said after he sat down at a marble-topped table and lit a cigar. "That's right. Shoo ... Shoo." For some reason I could not pronounce Shu Shan Sui correctly. It made me a little uneasy because it was only a Japanese word. But apparently he seemed indifferent and continued to talk of various things. About the novelist K; about a bulldog he had bought; about a poison gas called lewisite.

"You don't seem to be writing at all … I read 'Tenkibo.'[15] Was that your autobiography?"

"Yes. My autobiography."

"That was a bit morbid, you know. How are you now?"

"As usual, taking medicine all the time."

"I also have suffered from insomnia recently."

" 'I also.' Why do you say 'I also'?'

"But you said that you had insomnia, didn't you? Insomnia is dangerous, you know."

There was something close to a smile in his bloodshot left eye. I was aware that I could not pronounce the last syllable of 'insomnia' correctly.'[16] It's common enough with the son of a lunatic.

Within ten minutes I was again walking the streets alone. The bits of paper on the pavement seemed not unlike our human faces. Then a woman with bobbed hair appeared from the other direction. At a distance she was beautiful, but when she came directly before n~e, she appeared to be pregnant. I averted my face and turned into a wide side-street. Then presently I began to feel the pain of piles. The only cure for me was a sitz-bath … Beethoven also used a sitz-bath.

Immediately the sulphur used in the sitz-bath assailed my nostrils. But of course there in the street sulphur was nowhere visible. Once more I recalled the rose scraps of paper and walked firmly on.

An hour later I was ensconced in my room, my table facing the window, busy writing a new novel. My pen, in a way that was wonderful to me, ran swiftly over the paper. But after two or three hours it stopped as though seized by an invisible person. There was nothing I could do about it. I left the table and paced back and forth across the room. At times like this my megalomania was most marked. Filled with a savage joy, I felt that I had neither parents, wife nor children; I had only the life that flowed out of my pen.

But after four or five minutes I again had to face the telephone. I had answered it again and again; it only gave out vague words repeatedly. But one of them sounded like *mohru*. At length I left the phone and once more commenced pacing the room. But the word *mohru* stayed strangely in my mind.

Mohru was the Japanese word for "mole." This association was not pleasant for me. But in two or three seconds I changed the spelling of the word "mole" to *"la mort."* *Ra mohru* the French word for death immediately made me feel uneasy. As death oppressed my sister's husband so it oppressed me. But in the midst of my uneasiness I felt amused. I even smiled. Why had this amusement .come to me? I could not even guess. I stood for a long time in front of the mirror and looked straight at my reflection. Of course it was smiling. As I stared at it I thought of my second self. My second self—the German word "doppelganger"; fortunately I had never seen him. But the wife of K who had become an American movie actress had seen my second self in a corridor of the Imperial Theatre. (She had puzzled me by saying "I'm sorry I didn't greet you recently.") Then an old one-legged translator had also seen my self in a tobacconist's on the Ginza. Death might come to my second self rather than to me. If it came to me—I turned my back on the mirror and returned to my desk in front of the window.

The tuffa-framed panes overlooked a withered lawn and a pond. I remembered the notebooks and unfinished dramas which had been burned in the fire in the distant pine forest. Then I took my pen and started a new story.

V Red Glow

THE LIGHT of day made me suffer. Like a mole I lowered the blind, switched on the light and continued busily with my story. When I tired of the work I opened Tame's *Histoire de Literature Anglaise* and glanced at the lives of the poets. They were all unfortunate. The giants of the Elizabethan era: Ben Johnson, for instance, who watched the armies of Rome and Carthage join battle on his big toe and became a nervous wreck. I could not help feeling a crueljoy, full of malice, at their misfortunes.

One night when a strong east wind was blowing—a good omen for me—I went through the cellar into the street to call on an old man. He lived alone as a caretaker in the attic of a Bible society where he devoted himself to prayer and reading. We sat, our hands around the brazier, under a cross which hung on the wall, and talked of various things. Why did my mother go insane? Why did my father's business fail? Why was I being punished? He knew all these secrets. His face wreathed in its solemn smile he talked on and on, occasionally with pithy words which sketched a caricature from life. It was not that I did not respect this hermit of the attic. But as I talked to him I discovered that he also was driven by an affinity.

"That gardener's daughter is pretty. She's good-natured; she's very kind to me."

"How old is she?'

"Eighteen this year."

For all I knew it may have been only a fatherly love on his part. But I observed a gleam of passion in his eye. Not only that, the apple he offered me somehow revealed on its yellow skin the pattern of a one-horned beast. (I often saw mythical animals in the grain of wood or the cracks of coffee cups.) I recalled that a hostile critic had called me a unicorn child of the year 910,[17] and began to feel that this attic with its cross on the wall was not a place of refuge.

"How have you been recently?"

"Nerves jumpy as usual."

"Medicine won't help that. Haven't you any wish to become a believer?"

"If someone like me could become a believer."

"Oh, that's not difficult. Just believe in God, believe in Christ the Son of God. If only you believe the miracles that Christ performed …"

"Though I can believe in the devil."

"Then why don't you believe in God? If you believe in the shadow, you cannot help believing in the light, can you?'

"But there is darkness without light, isn't there?"

"What do you mean by that?'

I had nothing to say; he like me was walking in darkness. Our logic differed at only this one point. But for me at least it was a ditch I could not cross.

"There must be light and the evidence for it is that there are miracles. Miracles happen even now, you know."

"Those are miracles wrought by the devil."

"Why are you talking of the devil again?'

I felt tempted to tell him what had happened to me in the last year or two. But it was possible that he would tell it to my wife and children, and I was afraid that I like my mother would enter a mental hospital.

"What are those over there?"

The sturdy old man wheeled around to the bookshelves with a faun-like expression on his face.

"The complete works of Dostoevski. Have you read *Crime and Punishment*?"

Of course I had been familiar with several of Dostoevski's volumes from ten years back. But somehow the words *Crime and Punishment* struck me. I borrowed the volume and set out to return to my hotel room. Once again the busy sidewalks under the electric light seemed sinister to me. It would have been intolerable to meet an acquaintance. I deliberately chose the dark alleys and slunk along like a thief.

Before long I felt a pain in my stomach. Only a glass of whisky could alleviate this pain. I found a bar, opened the door and was about to enter, but in the tiny bar, thick with tobacco smoke, was a group of arty young men drinking sake. In their midst sat a girl with her hair over her ears earnestly playing the mandolin. Immediately I felt hesitation and turned back without entering. I discovered that my shadow was swaying from left to right and the light that lit me was a weird red. I stopped where I stood but my shadow went on swaying. Shakily I turned back to the bar and saw the colored glass lantern hanging from its eaves. It was swinging slowly in the strong wind.

I then entered a basement restaurant. I stood at the bar and ordered a whisky.

"Whisky? All we have is Black and White, sir."

I poured the whisky into the soda and drank it in silence, sip by sip. Beside me two men, thirtyish, who appeared to be newspaper reporters were talking in low voices—talking in French. I turned my back on them and felt their stares all over my body; my body tingled exactly as if they were electric waves. They must have known my face and heard rumours about me.

"Bien ... tres mauvais ... pourquoi?"

"Pourquoi? Le diable est mort."

"Oui, oui ... D'enfer."

I tossed a silver coin on the bar, the last I had and escaped from the place. The night breeze blowing down the street soothed the pain and healed my nerves. I recalled Raskolnikov and felt a strong urge to confess everything. But to do this to anyone except myself—to anyone outside my family would be tragedy. Moreover it was doubtful if this urge was sincere. If my nerves could be restored to sanity—but for that I would have to go away somewhere—to Madrid, to Rio, to Samarkand.

Presently a small white sign hanging from a shop front perturbed me. It was the trademark, a winged auto tire. I thought of the ancient Greek who launched himself on man-made wings. He soared into the sky, scorched his wings in the heat of the sun, fell and drowned in the sea ... To Madrid, to Rio, to Samarkand—I could not help sneering at my dreams and thought of Orestes pursued by the furies.

I walked by a canal in a side street. I remembered the house of my adoptive parents in the suburbs. Of course they must have been awaiting my return. Doubtless my children also—but if I went back to them I would fear the power of their fetters.[18] A barge swayed on the

31

waves of the canal. A feeble light leaked out low on its deck. Men and women were living there. Hating each other in order to love each other. I felt the warmth of the whisky, gathered my fighting spirit and returned to the hotel.

I sat down at my desk and resumed the reading of Merrimée's letters. Gradually they gave me the strength to go on living. But when I learned that Merrimée had become a Protestant towards the end of his life, I suddenly recalled his face in halfshadow. He, like us, was a man who walked in darkness. In darkness? *A Dark Night's Passing* began to be a terrifying book to me. In order to banish my gloom I picked up Anatole France's Dialogues and began to read it. But even the faun of our time was bearing a cross.[19]

An hour later a bellhop knocked to deliver a bundle of mail. One of the letters was from a Leipzig publisher asking me to write an essay on "The Modern Japanese Woman." Why would they ask me to write an essay like that? The letter was in English; a postscript in handwriting had been added: "We would be happy to have a picture in the Japanese style, in black and white—no colour—of a Japanese woman. I remembered the glass of Black and White whisky and tore the letter to shreds. Then I picked up another envelope at random, opened it and looked at yellow letter paper. It was from a young man whom I did not know. But before I had read two or three lines "Your 'Hell Screen' ..." irritated me. The third envelope I opened contained a letter from my nephew. I sighed in relief and read about family problems. But the conclusion hit me suddenly: "I am sending you the second edition of *Red Glow*."[20] Red glow! I felt a sardonic laugh coming and went to escape from the room. There was not a sign of anyone in the hall. Supporting myself with one hand against the wall, I walked with difficulty to the lobby. I sank down into a chair and lit a cigarette. It was an Airship. Since coming to the hotel I had been smoking nothing but Stars. Once again the manmade wings floated before my eyes. I called the bellhop from his corner and asked for two packs of Stars. But if he was to be believed, Stars were the only brand they were out of. "We have Airships, sir."

I shook my head and looked across the wide lobby. Opposite me four or five foreigners were sitting chatting around a table. One of them who wore a red one-piece dress was talking to the others but seemed to be looking at me from time to time.

"Mrs. Townshead."

Something I could not see was whispering this to me. Of course Mrs. Townshead was a name with which I was unfamiliar. Even if it was the name of that woman yonder—I rose from my chair and fearing that I might go mad returned to my room.

I had intended to ring a mental hospital as soon as I got back to my room. But to enter a hospital was to die. After an agony of hesitation I started to read *Crime and Punishment* in order to dispel my fear. But by chance I opened the book at a page with a sentence from "The Brothers Karamazov." Thinking I might have mistaken the book, I looked at the cover. *Crime and Punishment*; without doubt it was *Crime and Punishment*. Feeling that the bookbinder had made a mistake, and that it was the working of fate that I had opened the book at a mistaken insertion, I read on helplessly. But before I had read a page I felt my whole body shiver. It was a paragraph telling of the devil tormenting Ivan—Ivan—Strindberg—de Maupassant—or me here in this room.

Sleep alone could save me. But the last package of my sleeping pills was empty. I was quite unable to suffer on without sleep. Born of the courage of desperation, I had coffee brought up and like a dying madman pushed my pen. Two pages, five pages,—seven—ten—the manuscript progressed before my eyes. I was filling the story with supernatural creatures.[21] Fatigue was beclouding my head. At last I left the desk and lay down on the bed. I must have slept forty or fifty minutes. Then the feeling that someone was whispering "Le diable est mort" in my ears made me open my eyes.

The tuffa-framed window had opened to the chilly air. I paused in front of the door and surveyed the empty room, and doing so saw through the glass of the window, fogged by the outside air, a little landscape. Definitely it was a view of a pine forest with the sea beyond. Apprehensively I approached the window; I discovered that really it was the withered lawn and pond of the garden which formed the scene. But the illusion had awakened something close to nostalgia in me.

At nine o'clock I rang a certain magazine publisher, determined to return to my house as soon as I could get some money. I shoved the books and manuscript which were lying on the desk into my bag.

VI Airplane

I GOT off the train at a station on the Tokaido line and took a cab to the summer resort that lay beyond it. The driver was wearing a raincoat because of the cold. I

thought of the sinister omen and in order to avoid looking at him tried to keep looking out the window. Then I
saw passing along a piney depression—possibly an old
road—a funeral procession. There did not seem to be
any of the white dragon lanterns of a funeral but the
gold and silver artificial flowers were swaying in front
of and behind the coffin.

When at last I reached home, thanks to my wife and
children and sleeping pills I was able to spend two or
three days in tolerable peace. Our second floor looked
out on a pine forest with the sea in the distance. Seated
at the desk in this room, with the pigeons cooing in
my ears, I worked only in the forenoon. The birds—pigeons, crows, sparrows—flew up to the verandah. This
was most cheering to me and I remembered "Enter the
hall of the magpies[22] as I sat there pen in hand.

One hot sticky afternoon I set out under a cloudy
sky to buy ink at the general store. But all they had was
a row of sepia ink-bottles. I had always thought sepia
ink the most unpleasant of all colours. Since nothing
could be done about it, I came out into the street and
strolled along. There were few people around, but presently from the distance what appeared to be a foreigner
fortyish, came swaggering along. He was a Swede who
suffered from delusions of persecution. And to cap it all
his name was Strindberg. As I brushed by him I felt a
physical response.

The street was only two or three hundred yards
long. But in this short distance a dog that was half-black
approached me. As I turned a corner, I remembered
the Black and White whisky. Strindberg's tie was also
black and white. I felt that this could not be by chance.
If it were not by chance—I felt that it was only my head

which was walking and stopped briefly in the street. Inside a wire fence I could vaguely see a rainbow-coloured glass flower pot, abandoned. Around the bottom of this pot ran a raised wing-like pattern. Sparrows were fluttering down to it and back again to the top of a pine. As I approached the pot, all the sparrows as if by a pre-arranged signal flew up in the air.

I went to my wife's home and sat down in a cane chair that was in the front garden. Inside chicken-wire some white Leghorns were walking around quietly. A black dog was lying at my feet. Fretting to dispel the doubt that anyone could understand, outwardly at least I chatted with my mother-in-law and my wife's younger brother.[23]

"It's quiet here, isn't it."

"Quieter than Tokyo anyway."

"Do unpleasant things happen here also?'

"Well, after all this also is part of the world."

My mother-in-law laughed as she said this. Of course this also was a part of the "world." Well did I know how many tragedies and evils had happened here within one brief year. A doctor who had tried to kill one of his patients with slow poison; an old woman who had set fire to the house of her adopted son and daughter-in-law; a lawyer who had tried to steal his wife's property. When I saw the houses of these people I always felt that I was seeing hell in~the midst of life.

"There's one lunatic in town, isn't there?'

"You mean Mr. H. He's not a lunatic, he's only a man who became a fool."

"Dementia praecox, isn't it. When I see him I feel unbearably uncomfortable. A while ago I saw him bowing at the shrine of Batoh Kwanzeon."[24]

"Don't feel like that. You must become stronger. Though you, older brother, are stronger than I." My brother-in-law, hair untrimmed, sitting up on his bed, very reticent as usual, joined our conversation.

"There's always a weak spot in strength," I said.

"There now, don't say things like that." When my mother-in-law said this she was smiling bitterly. My brother-in-law was smiling also; gazing at the pine forest away beyond the fence he continued chatting casually. (After his illness he seemed to be pure spirit that had shed the flesh.)

"It's strange," he said, "When you think you have got away from being human, human desire becomes very violent."

"A good man may be a bad man, then?'

"Well, there are some people who are considered adults who are really children."

"No, it isn't that. No, it isn't that. I can't express it clearly. Something like the two poles opposed in electricity. Opposites combined in one."

The loud noise of an airplane startled us. Instinctively I looked up and saw a plane barely grazing the pine tops. Its wings were painted yellow; strangely enough, it was a monoplane.[25] The chickens and the dog were frightened and ran off in eight directions. The dog barked madly, put his tail between his legs and ran under the verandah.

"Won't it crash?'

"It's all right. Elder brother, do you know what 'aero-neurosis' is?"

"No."

"Well, because men who fly planes like that breathe the air of high space, they gradually come to feel they can't breathe the air of earth."

I left the house and walked through the pine forest in which not a twig was stirring. Gradually I became despondent. Why did that plane fly over my head instead of somewhere else? Why was there nothing but Airships on sale at that hotel. Suffering from many fears, I chose a deserted road.

The sea beyond the low sand dunes was a clouded red. A swing frame without swings stood there abruptly. I thought of the swing-frame and immediately thought of a gallows. Two or three crows were perched on the cross-piece. They stared at me but gave no sign of flying away. The crow in the middle stretched up its beak and cawed four times.[26]

I passed along the sandy embankment with its withered grass and turned down along the path along which stood many summer cottages. On the right of the path among the pines there should have been a white, two-storied house, Western-style. (A friend of mine had called it The House of Spring.) But when I passed there was only a bath and the concrete foundations. Afire, I thought immediately and passed it with averted head. A man on a bicycle riding straight towards me approached. He wore a dark brown cap and eyes fixed on the sand, pedalled along bent over the handlebars. Suddenly I believed his face was the face of my sister's husband, and before he reached where I was standing I slipped into a side-path. Here in the middle of the path was the putrescent corpse of a mole, its belly towards the sky.

At each step I felt that everything was being aimed at me. The half-transparent cogwheels one after another fell across my line of vision. Oppressed by the feeling that at last I had reached the end of my time, I walked on with head straight. As the cogwheels increased they suddenly began to whirl round. At the same time the branches in the pines on my right began to rustle; it was as though I were looking through cut-glass. I felt the palpitations of my heart increasing and stopped time after time on the path. But it was not easy to stop; I felt as though I were being pushed by somebody.

Thirty minutes later I lay on my back in an upstairs rooms in my house, my eyes shut tight and endured a frightful headache. Through my eyelids I began to see a wing with silvery feathers, a wing with silvery feathers arranged like scales. They were clearly to be seen on my retina. I opened my eyes and looked up at the ceiling but of course there was nothing like them on the ceiling. When I had satisfied myself about this, I closed my eyes again. But the silvery feathers were there in the darkness. Suddenly I remembered that there was a radiator cap with wings on a car in which I had ridden recently.

Someone ran up the stairs and ran clattering down again. I knew that this someone was my wife, got up quickly, surprised, and poked my head into the tearoom which was at the foot of the stairs. There was my wife, gasping for breath, her shoulders heaving.

"What's the matter?"

"Nothing." She raised her head and with a forced laugh continued, "Nothing's the matter. Nothing, really. It was just that I thought you were about to die."

That was the most terrible experience in my life. I have no strength to write any more. To go on living in the midst of feelings like this is intolerable. Isn't there someone who will be good enough to strangle me while I sleep?

NOTES

Notes that are translations of or based on Yoshida Seiichi's edition, one volume of selections, 1963, are indicated by the letter Y. (Truoka's essay, from which I have quoted, was printed in Alaska & Japan, *Alaska Methodist University Press, 1972.)*

1 The main railway line between Tokyo & Osaka.
2 A large bowl of rice, a meal in itself, cooked with chicken, egg & vegetables.
3 A large square of cloth, of various sizes, usually beautifully patterned, used for carrying things, tied at the four corners. Being supplanted today by plastic shopping bags.
4 A slang expression of the twenties and thirties, the Japanese pronunciation of "modern girl," sometimes shortened to "moga," the equivalent of the time to "hippy."
5 Conte. A crayon-type of picture named for its inventor, a French chemist. *Y.*
6 If it was not an illusion, the weird symbolism would disappear. If it was an illusion, it meant that the narrator's nerves were dangerously disordered. *Y.*
7 Akutagawa had frequently been to Aoyama Mental Hospital. It was run by Dr. Saito Shigeyoshi who was also a poet. Aoyarna Cemetery was nearby. Akutagawa consulted many doctors and was given many diagnoses. *Y.*
8 Still the largest and most famous bookstore in Japan, with many branches in big cities. The main store in Tokyo carries books in half a dozen languages beside Japanese.

9 A story from an ancient Chinese collection. The young man went to the capital of a neighbouring country, aped the manners of the citizens then returned to his native town. But he had forgotten the gait of his own people and really had not learned the ways of the capital. A parable of those who forget their duty and ape the manners of others. Falling between two stools. *Y.*

10 Akutagawa's given name was "Ryūnosuke" which means dragon-helper. *Y.*

11 The Empress Suiko's years were 593-628. *Y.*

12 The statue of Kusunoki Masashige. Legends made him one of the great loyalists fighting for the emperor, legends taught as history in school textbooks. But this was incorrect, as a scholar like Akutagawa knew. Hence the narrator's outburst. *Y.*

13 Shiga Naoya's autobiographical novel. *Y.*

14 Shu Shun Sui (1600-82) was a Chinese Confucian scholar. A retainer of the Ming dynasty, he immigrated to Japan, became a Japanese subject in 1660 and joined the Mito clan on the invitation of its head, Tokugawa Mitsukuni. In 1912 a memorial stone to him in the grounds of the First Higher School (what Westerners call a junior college), formerly the Tokyo seat of the Mito clan was erected. Akutagawa was in his second year at the college where it was erected. Now it is part of Tokyo University. *Y.*

15 "Tenkibo," a short story, appeared in the November number of the magazine *Kaizo*. It was a sort of memoir of the deaths of Akutagawa's father, mother and older sister. It begins "My mother was a lunatic," describes his mother who died insane, the early death of his sister and of his father who became insane before he died. *Y.*

16 The Japanese word for insomnia is "fuminshoh."

¹⁷ A Kirinji, a unicorn-child is a wunderkind. The hostile critic was sneering at Akutagawa's adolescent fame; 910 was a scarcely disguised reference to the second decade of the 20th century. However Akutagawa did not receive prominence till the publication of a collection of short stories entitled *Rashomon* in 1917. *Y.*

¹⁸ The bonds of wife and children; the bonds of affection and the weight of the feudal family system. *Y.*

¹⁹ Akutagawa personified the modern spirit as a faun bearing a cross, i.e. one who is doomed to martyrdom. *Y.*

²⁰ *Red Glow,* the first book of poems by Dr. Saito Shigeyoshi, one of the psychiatrists who treated Akutagawa. The first edition appeared in 1913 and was reprinted in 1921. The poems depicted the sorrows of modern man and evoked a great response. Some of the poems tell of the mentally ill. Akutagawa speaks of reading "Red Glow" when he was in junior college. Here it is partly the colour of the letter-paper which distresses Akutagawa. *Y.*

²¹ Akutagawa was writing *Kappa,* the story about Japanese kelpies. It was finished in the middle of February and published in March 1927. "In describing one of these creatures I was describing myself," wrote Akutagawa. The creature is Tokku, a Kappa poet who commits suicide in the story. The writer was contemplating his own suicide when he doomed Tokku to self-slaughter. *Y.*

²² Magpies are supposed to bring happiness. *Y.*

²³ His name was Tsukamoto *Ya*esu, his house was in Kugenuma. He was convalescing from tuberculosis.

²⁴ Batoh Kwanzeon or Kwannon, a god with a crowned horse's head and three faces of fury who subdues earthly passions. *Y.*

[25] Icarus; man-made wings again. **Y.**

[26] Four is a word of ill omen in Japan because in one of its common readings, "She," it is a homonym of "death," "shi."

Hell Screen

I DOUBT WHETHER THERE WILL EVER BE ANOTHER MAN like the Lord of Horikawa. Certainly there has been no one like him till now. Some say that a Guardian King appeared to her ladyship his mother in a dream before he was born; at least it is true that from the day he was born he was a most extraordinary person. Nothing he did was commonplace; he was constantly startling people. You have only to glance at a plan of Horikawa to perceive its grandeur. No ordinary person would ever have dreamt of the boldness and daring with which it was conceived.

But it certainly was not his lordship's intention merely to glorify himself; he was generous, he did not forget the lower classes; he wanted the whole country to enjoy itself when he did.

There is the story about the famous Kawâra Palace at Higashi Sanjo. It was said that the ghost of Toru, Minister of the Left, appeared there night after night until his lordship exorcised it by rebuking it. Such was his prestige in the capital that everyone, man, woman, and girl, regarded him, with good reason, as a god incarnate. Once, as he was returning in his carriage from the Feast of the Plum Blossoms, his ox got loose and injured an old man who happened to be passing. But the latter, they say, put his hands together in reverence and was actually grateful that he had been knocked over by an ox of his lordship.

Thus, there are the makings of many good stories in the life of his lordship. At a certain banquet he made a presentation of thirty white horses; another time he gave a favourite boy to be the human pillar of Nagara Bridge. There would be no end if I started to tell them all. Numerous as these anecdotes are, I doubt if there are any that match in horror the story of the making of the Hell Screen, one of the most valuable treasurea in the house. His lordship is not easily upset, but that time he seemed to be startled. How much more terrified, then, were we who served him; we feared for our very souls. As for me, I had served him for twenty years, but when I witnessed that dreadful spectacle I felt that such a thing could never have happened before. But in order to tell this story, I must first tell about Yoshihide, who painted the Hell Screen.

2

YOSHIHIDE IS, I expect, remembered by many even today. In his time he was a famous painter surpassed by no contemporary. He would be about fifty then, I imagine. He was cross-grained, and not much to look at: short of stature, a bag of skin and bones, and his youthful red lips made him seem even more evil, as though he were some sort of animal. Some said it was because he put his reddened paint brush to his lips, but I doubt this. Others, more unkind, said that his appearance and movements suggested a monkey. And that reminds me of this story. Yoshihide's only daughter, Yuzuki, a charming girl of fifteen, quite unlike her father, was at that time a maid in Horikawa. Probably owing to the fact that her mother had died while she was still very small,Yuzuki was sympathetic and intelligent beyond her years, and greatly petted by her ladyship and her attendants in consequence.

About that time it happened that someone presented a tame monkey from Tamba. The mischievous young lord called it Yoshihide. The monkey was a comical-looking beast, anyway; with this name, nobody in the mansion could resist laughing at him. But they did more than that. If he climbed the pine tree in the garden, or soiled the mats, whatever he did they teased him, shouting, "Yoshihide, Yoshihide."

One day Yuzuki was passing along one of the long halls with a note in a twig of red winter plum blossom when the monkey appeared from behind a sliding door, fleeing as fast as he could. Apparently he had dislocated a leg, for he limped, unable, it seemed, to climb a post with his usual agility. After him came the young ,lord, waving a switch, shouting, "Stop thief! Orange thief!" Yuzuki hesitated a moment, but it gave the fleeing monkey a chance to cling to her skirt, crying most piteously. Suddenly she felt she could not restrain her pity. With one hand she still held the plum branch, with the other, the sleeve of her mauve kimono sweeping in a half-circle, she picked the monkey up gently. Then bending before the young lord, she said sweetly, "I crave your pardon. He is only an animal. Be kind enough to pardon him, my lord."

But he had come running with his temper up; he frowned and stamped his foot two or three times. "Why do you protect him? He has stolen some oranges."

"But he is only an animal." She repeated it; then after a little, smiling sadly, "And since you call him Yoshihide, it is as if my father were being punished. I couldn't bear to see it," she said boldly. This defeated the young lord.

"Well, if you're pleading for your father's skin, I'll pardon him," he said reluctantly, "against my better judgement." Dropping the switch, he turned and went back through the sliding door through which he had come.

3

YUZUKI AND the monkey were devoted to each other from that day. She hung a golden bell that she had received from the Princess by a bright red cord around the monkey's neck, and the monkey would hardly let her out of his sight. Once, for instance, when she caught cold and took to her bed, the monkey, apparently much depressed, sat immovable by her pillow, gnawing his nails.

Another strange thing was that from that time the monkey was not teased as badly as before. On the contrary, they began to pet him, and even the young lord would occasionally toss him a persimmon or a chestnut. Once he got quite angry when he caught a samurai kicking the monkey. As for his lordship, they say that when he heard his son was protecting the monkey from abuse, he had Yuzuki appear before him with the monkey in her arms. On this occasion he must have heard why she had made a pet of the monkey.

"You're a filial girl. I'll reward you for it," he said, and gave her a crimson ceremonial kimono. Whereupon the monkey with the greatest deference mimicked her acceptance of the kimono. That greatly tickled his lordship, because he admired her filial piety—not, as rumour had it, because he was too fond of her. There may have been some grounds for this rumour, but of that I shall tell later. It should be enough to say that the Lord of Horikawa was not the sort of person to fall in love with an artist's daughter, no matter how beautiful she was.

Thus honoured, Yoshihide's daughter withdrew from his presence. Since she was wise and good, the other maids were not jealous of her. Rather she and her monkey became more popular than ever, particularly, they say, with the Princess, from whom she was hardly ever separated. She invariably accompanied her in her pleasure carriage.

However, we must leave the daughter a while and turn to the father. Though the monkey was soon being petted by everybody, they all disliked the great Yoshihide. This was not limited to the mansion folk only. The Abbot of Yogogawa hated him, and if Yoshihide were mentioned would change colour as though he had encountered a devil. (That was after Yoshihide had drawn a caricature of the Abbot, according the the gossip of the domestics, which, after all, may have been nothing more than gossip.) Anyhow, the man was unpopular with anyone you met. If there were some who did not speak badly of him, they were but two or three fellow-artists or people who knew his pictures, but not the man.

Yoshihide was not only very repellent in appearance: people disliked him more because of his habits. No one was to blame for his unpopularity except himself.

4

HE WAS stingy, he was bad-tempered, he was shameless, he was lazy, he was greedy, but worst of all, he was arrogant and contemptuous, certain that he was the greatest artist in the country.

If he had been proud only of his work it would not have been so bad, but he despised everything, even the customs and amenities of society.

It was in character, therefore, that when he was making a picture of the Goddess of Beauty he should paint the face of a common harlot, and that for Fudo[1] he should paint a villainous ex-convict. The models he chose were shocking. When he was taken to task for it, he said coolly, "It would be strange if the gods and buddhas I have given life with my brush should punish me."

His apprentices were appalled when they thought of the dreadful fate in store for him, and many left his studio. It was pride—he imagined himself to be the greatest man in Japan.

In short, though exceptionally gifted, he behaved much above his station. Among artists who were not on good terms with him, many maintained that he was a charlatan, because his brushwork and coloring were so unusual. Look at the door-paintings of the famous artists of the past! You can almost smell the perfume of the plum blossom on a moonlit night; you can almost hear some courtier on a screen playing his flute. That is how they gained their reputation for surpassing beauty. Yoshihide's pictures were reputed to be always weird or unpleasant. For instance, he painted the "Five Aspects of Life and Death" on Ryugai Temple gate, and they say if you pass the gate at night you can hear the sighing and sobbing of the divinities depicted there. Others say you can smell rotting corpses. Or when, at the command of his lordship, he painted the portraits of some of his household women, within three years everyone of them sickened as though her spirit had left her, and died. Those who spoke ill of Yoshihide regarded this as certain proof that his pictures were done by means of the black art.

Yoshihide delighted in his reputation for perversity. Once, when his lordship said to him jokingly, "You seem to like the ugly," Yoshihide's unnaturally red lips curled in an evil laugh. "I do. Daubers usually cannot understand the beauty of ugly things," he said contemptuously.

But Yoshihide, the unspeakably unscrupulous Yoshihide, had one tender human trait.

5

AND THAT was his affection for his only child, whom he loved passionately. As I said before, Yuzuki was gentle, and deeply devoted to her father, but his love for her was not inferior to her devotion to him. Does it not seem incredible that the man who never gave a donation to a temple could have provided such kimono and hairpins for his daughter with reckless disregard of cost?

But Yoshihide's affection for Yuzuki was nothing more than the emotion. He gave no thought for instance, to finding her a good husband. Yet he certainly would have hired roughs to assassinate anyone who made improper advances to her. Therefore, when she became a maid at Horikawa, at the command of his lordship, Yoshihide took it very badly; and even when he appeared before the daimyo, he sulked for a while. The rumor that, attracted by her beauty, his lordship had tasted her delights in spite of her father, was largely the guess of those who noted Yoshihide's displeasure.

Of course, even if the rumour were false it was clear that the intensity of his affection made Yoshihide long to have his daughter come down from among his lordship's women. When Yoshihide was commanded to paint Monju, the God of Wisdom, he took as his model his lordship's favourite page, and the Lord of Horikawa, highly pleased—for it was a beautiful thing—said graciously, "I will give you whatever you wish as a reward. Now what would you like?" Yoshihide acknowledged the tribute; but what do you think was the bold request that he made? That his daughter should leave his lordship's service! It would be presumptuous to ask that one's daughter be taken in; who but Yoshihide would have asked for his daughter's release, no matter how much he loved her! At this even the genial daimyo seemed ruffled, and he silently watched Yoshihide's face for a long moment.

"No," he spat out, and stood up suddenly. This happened again on four or five different occasions, and as I recall it now, with each repetition, the eye with which his lordship regarded Yoshihide grew colder. Possibly it was on account of this that Yuzuki was concerned for her father's safety, for often, biting her sleeves, she sobbed when she was in her room. Without doubt it was this that made the rumours that his lordship had fallen in love with Yoshihide's daughter become widely current. One of them had it that the very existence of the Hell Screen was owing to the fact that she would not comply with his wishes, but of course this could not have been true.

We believe his lordship did not dismiss her simply because he pitied her. He felt sorry for her situation, and rather than leave her with her hardened father he wanted her in the mansion where there would be no inconvenience for her. It was nothing but kindness on his part. It was quite obvious that the girl received his favours, but it would have been an exaggeration to say that she was his mistress. No, that would have been a completely unfounded lie.

Be that as it may, owing to his request about his daughter, Yoshihide came to be disliked by his lordship. Then suddenly the Lord of Horikawa summoned Yoshihide, whatever may have been his reason and bade him paint a screen of the circles of hell.

6

WHEN I say screen of the circles of hell, the scenes of those frightful paintings seem to come floating before my very eyes. Other painters have done Hell Screens, but from the first sketch Yoshihide's was different. In one corner of the first leaf he painted the Ten Kings[2] and their households in small scale, the rest was an awful whirlpool of fire around the Forest of Swords which likewise seemed ready to burst into flames. In fact, except for the robes of the hellish officials, which were dotted yellows, all was a flame colour, and in the center leapt and danced pitch-black smoke and sparks like flying charcoal.

The brushwork of this alone was enough to astonish one, but the treatment of the sinners rolling over and over in the avenging fire was unlike that of any ordinary picture of hell. From the highest noble to the lowest beggar every conceivable sort of person was to be seen there. Courtiers in formal attire, alluring young maidens of the court in palace robes, priests droning over their prayer beads, scholars on high wooden clogs, little girls in white shifts, diviners flourishing their papered wands—I won't name them all. There they all were, enveloped in flame and smoke, tormented by bull- and horse-headed jailers: blown and scattered in all directions like fallen leaves in a gale, they fled hither and yon. There were female fortunetellers, their hair caught in forks, their limbs trussed tighter than spiders' legs. Young princes hung inverted like bats, their breasts pierced with javelins. They were beaten with iron whips, they were crushed with mighty weights of adamant, they were pecked by weird birds, they were devoured by poisonous dragons. I don't know how many sinners were depicted, nor can I list all their torments.

But I must mention one dreadful scene that stood out from the rest. Grazing the tops of the sword trees, that were as sharp as an animal's fangs—there were several souls on them, spitted two or three deep—caine falling through space an ox-carriage. Its blinds were blown open by the winds of hell and in it an emperor's favorite, gorgeously attired, her long black hair fluttering in the flames, bent her white neck and writhed in agony. Nothing made the fiery torments of hell more realistic than the appearance of that woman in her burning carriage. The horror of the whole picture was concentrated in this one scene. So inspired an accomplishment was it that those who looked at her thought they heard dreadful cries in their ears.

Ah, it was for this, it was for this picture that that dreadful event occurred! Without it how could even Yoshihide have expressed so vividly the agonies of hell? It was to finish this screen that Yoshihide met a destiny so cruel that he took his own life. For this hell he pictured was the hell that he, the greatest painter in the country, was one day to fall into ...

I may be telling the strange story of the Hell Screen too hastily; I may have told the wrong end of the story first. Let me return to Yoshihide, bidden by his lordship to paint a picture of hell.

7

FOR FIVE or six months Yoshihide was so busy working on the screen that he was not seen at the mansion at all. Was it not remarkable that with all his affection, when he became absorbed in his painting, he did not even want to see his daughter? The apprentice to whom I have already referred said that when Yoshihide was engaged on a piece of work it was as though he had been bewitched by a fox. According to the stories that circulated at that time Yoshihide had achieved fame with the assistance of the black art because of a vow he had made to some great god of fortune. And the proof of it was that if you went to his studio and peered at him unbeknownst you could see the ghostly foxes swarming all around him. Thus it was that when once he had taken up his brushes everything was forgotten till he had finished the picture. Day and night he would shut himself up in one room, scarcely seeing the light of day. And when he painted the Hell Screen this absorption was complete.

The shutters were kept down during the day and he mixed his secret colours by the light of a tripod lamp. He had his apprentices dress in all sorts of finery, and painted each with great care. It did not take the Hell Screen to make him behave like that: he demanded it for every picture he painted. At the time he was painting the "Five Aspects of Life and Death" at Ryugaiji, he chanced to see a corpse lying beside the road. Any ordinary person would have averted his face, but Yoshihide stepped out of the crowd, squatted down, and at his leisure painted the half-decayed face and limbs exactly as they looked.

How can I convey his violent concentration? Some of you will still fail to grasp it. Since I cannot tell it in detail, I shall relate it broadly.

The apprentice then, was one day mixing paints. Suddenly Yoshihide appeared. "I'd like to take a short nap," he said. "But I've been bothered a lot by bad dreams recently."

Since this was not extraordinary the apprentice answered briefly but politely, "Indeed, sir," without lifting his hand from his work. Whereupon the artist said, with a loneliness and diffidence that were strange to him, "I mean I would like to have you sit by my pillow while I rest." The apprentice thought it unusual that he should be troubled so badly by dreams, but the request was a simple one and he assented readily. Yoshihide, still anxious, asked him to come back in at once. "And if another apprentice comes, don't let him enter the room while I am sleeping," he said hesitantly. By "room" he meant the room where he was painting the screen. In that room the doors were shut fast as if it were night, and a light was usually left burning. The screen stood around the sides of the room; only the charcoal sketch of the design was completed. Yoshihide put his elbow on the pillow like a man completely exhausted and quietly fell asleep. But before an hour was out an indescribably unpleasant voice began to sound in the apprentice's ears.

8

AT FIRST it was nothing more than a voice, but presently there were clear words, as of a drowning man moaning in the water. "What you are calling me? Where? Where to ... to hell? To the hell of fire Who is it? Who is your honour? Who is your honour? If I knew who ..."

Unconsciously the apprentice stopped mixing the colours; feeling that he was intruding on privacy he looked at the artist's face. That wrinkled face was pale; great drops of sweat stood out on it, the lips were dry, and the mouth with its scanty teeth was wide open, as though it gasped for air. And that thing that moved so dizzily as if on a thread, was that his tongue!

"If I knew who ... Oh, it is your honour, is it? I thought it was. What! You have come to meet me. So I am to come. I am to go to hell! My daughter awaits me in hell!"

At that moment a strange, hazy shadow seemed to descend over the face of the screen, so uncanny did the apprentice feel. Immediately, of course, he shook the master with all his might, but Yoshihide, still in the clutch of the nightmare, continued his monologue, unable, apparently, to wake out of it. Thereupon the apprentice boldly took the water that stood at hand for his brushes and poured it over Yoshihide's face.

"It is waiting: get in this carriage. Get in this carriage and go down to hell." As he said these words Yoshihide's voice changed, he sounded like a man being strangled, and at length he opened his eyes. Terrified, he leapt up like one pierced with needles: the weird things of his dream must still have been with him. His expression was dreadful, his mouth gaped, he stared into space. Presently he seemed to have recovered himself. "It's all right now. You may leave," he said curtly.

As the apprentice would have been badly scolded had he disobeyed, he promptly left the room. When he saw the good light of day, he sighed with relief like one awakening from a bad dream.

But this was not the worst. A month later another apprentice was called into the back room. As usual Yoshihide was gnawing his brushes in the dim light of the oil lamp. Suddenly he turned to the apprentice. "I want you to strip again."

Since he had been asked to do this several times before, the apprentice obeyed immediately. But when that unspeakable man saw him stark naked before him, his face became strangely distorted. "I want to see a man bound with a chain. I want you to do as I tell you for a little while," he said coldly and unsympathetically. The apprentice was a sturdy fellow who had formerly thought that swinging a sword was better than handling a brush, but this request astonished him. As he often said afterwards, "I began to wonder if the master hadn't gone crazy and wasn't going to kill me." Yoshihide, however, growing impatient with the other's hesitation, produced from somewhere a light iron chain a-rattle in his hand; and without giving him the opportunity of obeying or refusing, sprang on the apprentice, sat on his back, twisted up his arms and bound him around and around. The pain was almost intolerable, for he pulled the end of the chain brutally, so that the apprentice fell loudly sideways and lay there extended.

9

HE SAID that he lay there like a wine jar rolled over on its side. Because his hands and feet were cruelly bent and twisted he could move only his head. He was fat, and with his circulation impeded, the blood gathered not only in his trunk and face but everywhere under his skin. This, however, did not trouble Yoshihide at all; he walked all around him, "a wine jar," making sketch after sketch. I do not need to elaborate on the apprentice's sufferings.

Had nothing occurred, doubtless the torture would have been protracted longer. Fortunately—or maybe unfortunately—something like black oil, a thin streak, came flowing sinuously from behind a jar in the corner of the room. At first it moved slowly like a sticky substance, but then it slid more smoothly until, as he watched it, it moved gleamingly up to his nose. He drew in his breath involuntarily. "A snake! A snake!" he screamed. It seemed that all the blood in his body would freeze at once, nor was it surprising. A little more and the snake would actually have touched with its cold tongue his head into which the chains were biting. Even the unscrupulous Yoshihide must have been startled at this. He dropped his brush, bent down like a flash, deftly caught t~he snake by its tail and lifted it up, head downward. The snake raised its head, coiled itself in circles, twisted its body, but could not reach Yoshihide's hand.

"You have made me botch a stroke." Complaining offensively, Yoshihide dropped the snake into the jar in the corner of the room and reluctantly loosed the chain that bound the apprentice. All he did was to loose him; not a word of thanks did the long-suffering fellow get. Obviously Yoshihide was vexed that he had botched a stroke instead of letting his apprentice be bitten by the snake. Afterwards they heard that he kept the snake there as a model.

This story should give you some idea of Yoshihide's madness, his sinister absorption. However, I should like to describe one more dreadful experience that almost cost a young apprentice his life. He was thirteen or fourteen at the time, a girlish, fair-complexioned lad. One night he was suddenly called to his master's room. In the lamplight he saw Yoshihide feeding a strange bird, about the size of an ordinary cat, with a bloody piece of meat which he held in his hand. It had large, round, amber-coloured eyes and feather-like ears that stuck out on either side of its head. It was extraordinarily like a cat.

10

YOSHIHIDE ALWAYS disliked anyone sticking his nose into what he was doing. As was the case with the snake, his apprentices never knew what he had in his room. Therefore sometimes silver bowls, sometimes a skull, or one-stemmed lacquer stands—various odd things, models for what he was painting—would be set out on his table. But nobody knew where he kept these things. The rumour that some great god of fortune lent him divine help certainly arose from these circumstances.

Then the apprentice, seeing the strange bird on the table and imagining it to be something needed for the Hell Screen, bowed to the artist and said respectfully, "What do you wish, sir?" Yoshihide, as if he had not heard him, licked his red lips and jerked his chin towards the bird. "Isn't it tame!"

While he was saying this the apprentice was staring with an uncanny feeling at that catlike bird with ears. Yoshihide answered with his sneer, "What! Never seen a bird like this? That's the trouble with people who live in the capital. It's a horned owl. A hunter gave it to me two or three days ago. But I'll warrant there aren't many as tame as this."

As he said this he slowly raised his hand and stroked the back of the bird, which had just finished eating the meat, the wrong way. The owl let out a short piercing screech, flew up from the table, extended its claws, and pounced at the face of the apprentice. Panicstricken, the latter raised his sleeve to shield his face. Had he not done so he undoubtedly would have been badly slashed. As he cried out he shook his sleeve to drive off the owl, but it screeched and, taking advantage of his weakness, attacked again. Forgetting the master's presence, the lad fled distracted up and down the narrow room; standing, he tried to ward it off, sitting, to drive it away. The sinister bird wheeled high and low after its prey, darting at his eyes, watching for an opening. The noisy threshing of its wings seemed to evoke something uncanny like the smell of dead leaves, or the spray of a waterfall. It was dreadful, revolting. The apprentice had the feeling that the dim oil lamp was the vague light of the moon, and the room a valley shut in the ill-omened air of some remote mountain.

But the apprentice's horror was due not so much to the attack of the horned owl. What made his hair stand on end was the sight of the artist Yoshihide. The latter watched the commotion coolly, unrolled his paper deliberately, and began to paint the fantastic picture of a girlish boy being mangled by a horrible bird. When the apprentice saw this out of the corner of his eye, he was overwhelmed with an inexpressible horror, for he thought that he really was going to be killed for the artist.

11

YOU COULD say that this was impossible to believe. Yoshihide had called the apprentice deliberately that night in order to set the owl after him and paint him trying to escape. Therefore the apprentice, when he saw what the master was up to, involuntarily hid his head in his sleeves, began screaming he knew not what, and huddled down in the corner of the room by the sliding door. Then Yoshihide shouted as though he were a little flustered and got to his feet, but immediately the beating of the owl's wings became louder and there was the startling noise of things being torn or knocked down. Though he was badly shaken, the apprentice involuntarily lifted his head to see. The room had become as black as night, and out of it came Yoshihide's voice harshly calling for his apprentices.

Presently one of them answered from a distance, and in a minute came running in with a light. By its sooty illumination he saw the tripod lamp overturned and the owl fluttering painfully with one wing on mats that were swimming in oil. Yoshihide was in a halfsitting position beyond the table. He seemed aghast and was muttering words unintelligible to mortals. This is no exaggeration. A snake as black as the pit was coiling itself rapidly around the owl, encircling its neck and one wing. Apparently in crouching down the apprentice had knocked over the jar, the snake had crawled out, and the owl had made a feeble attempt to pounce on it. It was this which had caused the clatter and commotion. The two apprentices exchanged glances and simply stood dumbfounded, eyeing that remarkable spectacle. Then without a word they bowed to Yoshihide and withdrew. Nobody discovered what happened to the owl and the snake.

This sort of thing was matched by many other incidents. I forgot to say that it was in the early autumn that Yoshihide received orders to paint the screen. From then until the end of the winter his apprentices were in a constant state of terror because of his weird behaviour. But towards the end of the winter something about the picture seemed to trouble Yoshihide; he became even more saturnine than usual and spoke more harshly. The sketch of the screen, eight-tenths completed, did not progress. In fact, there did not seem to be any chance that the outlines would ever be painted in and finished.

Nobody knew what it was that hindered the work on the screen and nobody tried to find out. Hitherto the apprentices had been fascinated by everything that happened. They had felt that they were caged with a wolf or a tiger, but from this time they contrived to keep away from their master as much as possible.

12

ACCORDINGLY, THERE is not much that is worth telling about this period. But if one had to say something, it would be that the stubborn old man was, for some strange reason, easily moved to tears, and was often found weeping, they say, when he thought no one was by. One day, for instance, an appr.entice went into the garden on an errand. Yoshihide was standing absently in the corridor, gazing at the sky with its promise of spring, his eyes full of tears. The apprentice felt embarassed and withdrew stealthily without saying a word. Was it not remarkable that the arrogant man who had used a decaying corpse as model for the "Five Aspects of Life and Death" should weep so childishly?

While Yoshihide painted the screen in a frenzy incomprehensible to the sane, it began to be noticed that his daughter was very despondent and often appeared to be holding back tears. When this happens to a girl with a pale modest face, her eyelashes become heavy, shadows appear around her eyes, and her face grows still sadder. At first they said that she was suffering from a love affair, or blamed her father, but soon it got around that the Lord of Horikawa wanted to have his way with her. Then suddenly all talk about the girl ceased as if everybody had forgotten her.

It was about that time that late one night I happened to be passing along a corridor. Suddenly the monkey

Yoshihide sprang out from somewhere and began pulling the hem of my skirt insistently. As I remember it, the night was warm, there was a pale moon shining, and the plum blossoms were already fragrant. The monkey bared his white teeth, wrinkled the tip of his nose, and shrieked wildly in the moonlight as though he were demented. I felt upset and very angry that my new skirts should be pulled about. Kicking the monkey loose, I was about to walk on when I recalled that a samurai had earned the young lord's displeasure by chastising the monkey. Besides his behaviour did seem most unusual. So at last I walked a dozen yards in the direction he was pulling me.

Tbere the corridor turned, showing the water of the pond, pale white in the night light, beyond a pine tree with gently bending branches. At that point what sounded like people quarreling fell on my ears, weird and startling, from a room nearby. Except for this everything around was sunk in silence. In the half-light that was neither haze nor moonlight I heard no other voices. There was nothing but the sound of the fish jumping in the pond. With that din in my ears, I stopped instinctively. My first thought was "Some ruffians," and I approached the sliding door quietly, holding my breath, ready to show them my mettle.

13

BUT THE monkey must have thought me too hesitant. He ran around me two or three times, impatiently, crying out as though he were being strangled, then leapt straight up from the floor to my shoulder. I jerked back my head so as not to be clawed, but he clung to my sleeve to keep from falling to the floor. Staggering back two or three steps, I banged heavily into the sliding door. After that there was no cause for hesitatimi. I opened the door immediately and was about to advance into the inner part of the room where the moonlight did not fall. But just then something passed before my eyes—what was this?—a girl came running out from the back of the room as though released from a spring. She barely missed running into me, passed me, and half-fell outside the room, where she knelt gasping, looking up at my face, and shuddering as though she still saw some horror.

Do I need to say she was Yuzuki? That night she appeared vivid, she seemed to be a different person. Her big eyes shone, her cheeks flamed red. Her disordered kimono and skirt gave her a fascination she did not ordinarily possess. Was this really that shrinking daughter of Yoshihide's? I leaned against the sliding door and stared at her beautiful figure in the moonlight. Then, indicating the direction where the alarmed footsteps had died away, "What was it?" I asked with my eyes.

But she only bit her lips, shook her head, and said nothing. She seemed unusually mortified. Then I bent over her, put my mouth to her ear, and asked, "Who was it?" in a whisper. But the girl still shook her head; tears filled her eyes and hung on her long lashes; she bit her lips harder than ever.

I have always been a stupid person and unless something is absolutely plain I cannot grasp it. I did not know what to say and stood motionless for a moment, as though listening to the beating of her heart. But this was because I felt I ought not to question her too closely.

I don't know how long it lasted. At length I closed the door I had left open and, looking back at the girl, who seemed to have recovered from her agitation, said as gently as possible, "You had better go back to your room." Then, troubled with the uncomfortable feeling that I had seen something I should not have, embarassed no one was near, I quietly returned to where I had come from. But before I had gone ten steps, something again plucked the hem of my skirt, tinidly this time. Astonished, I stopped and turned around. What do you think it was? The monkey Yoshihide, his gold bell jingling, his hands together like a human, was bowing most politely to me, again and again.

14

ABOUT TWO weeks later Yoshihide came to the mansion and asked for an immediate audience with the Lord of Horikawa. He belonged to the lower classes but he had always been in favour, and his lordship, ordinarily difficult of access, granted Yoshihide an audience at once. The latter prostrated himself before the daimyo deferentially and presently began to speak in his hoarse voice.

"Some time ago, my lord, you ordered a Hell Screen. Day and night have I laboured, taking great pains, and now the result can be seen: the design has almost been completed."

"Congratulations. I am content." But in his lordship's voice there was a strange lack of conviction, of interest.

"No, congratulations are not in order." With his eyes firmly lowered Yoshihide answered almost as if he were becoming angry. "It is nearly finished, but there is just one part I cannot paint—now."

"What! You cannot paint part of it!"

"No, my lord. I cannot paint anything for which a model is lacking. Even if I try, the pictures lack conviction. And isn't that the same as being unable to paint it?"

When he heard this a sneering sort of smile passed over his lordship's face. "Then in order to paint this Hell Screen, you must see hell, eh?"

"Yes, my lord. Some years ago in a great fire I saw flames close up that resembled the raging fires of hell. The flames in my painting are what I then saw. Your lordship is acquainted with that picture, I believe."

"What about criminals? You haven't seen jailers, have you?" he spoke as though he had not heard Yoshihide, his words following the artist's without pause.

"I have seen men bound in iron chains. I have copied in detail men attacked by strange birds. So I cannot say I have not seen the sufferings of criminals under torture. As for jailers—" Yoshihide smiled repulsively, "I have seen them before me many times in my dreams. Cows' heads, horses' heads, three-faced six-armed demons, clapping hands that make no noise, voiceless mouths agape—they all come to torment me. I am not exaggerating when I say that I see them every day and every night. What I wish to paint and cannot are not things like that."

His lordship must have been thoroughly astonished. For a long moment he stared at Yoshihide irritably; then he arched his eyebrows sharply. "What is it you cannot paint?"

15

"IN THE middle of the screen I want to paint a carriage falling down through the sky," said Yoshihide, and for the first time he looked sharply at his lordship's face. When Yoshihide spoke of pictures I have heard that he looked insane. He-certainly seemed insane when he said this. "In the carriage an exquisite court lady, her hair disordered in the raging fire, writhes in agony. Her face is contorted with smoke, her eyebrows are drawn; she looks up at the roof of the carriage, as she plucks at the bamboo blinds she tries to ward off the sparks that shower down. And strange birds of prey, ten or twenty, fly around the carriage with shrill cries. Ah, the beauty in the carriage. I cannot possibly paint her."

"Well, what else?"

For some reason his lordship took strange pleasure in urging Yoshihide on. But the artist's red lips moved feverishly, and when he spoke it was like a man in a dream. "No," he repeated, "I cannot paint it." Then suddenly he almost snarled, "Burn a carriage for me. If only you could …"

His lordship's face darkened, then he burst out laughing with startling abruptness. "I'll do entirely as you wish," he said, almost choking with the violence of his laughter. "And all discussion as to whether it is possible or not is beside the point."

When I heard this I felt a strange thrill of horror. Maybe it was a premonition. His lordship, as though infected with Yoshihide's madness, changed, foam gathered white on his lips, and like lightning the terror flashed in the corners of his eyes. He stopped abruptly, and then a great laugh burst from his throat. "I'll fire a carriage for you. And there'll be an exquisite beauty in the robes of a fine lady in it. Attacked by flames and black smoke the woman will die in agony. The man who thought of painting that must be the greatest artist in Japan. I'll praise him. Oh, I'll praise him!"

When he heard his lordship's words, Yoshihide became pale and moved his lips as though he we were gasping. But soon his body relaxed, and placing both hands on the mats, he bowed politely. "How kind a destiny," he said, so low that he could scarcely be heard. Probably this was because the daimyo's words had brought the frightfulness of his plan vividly before his eyes. That was the only time in my life that I pitied Yoshihide.

16

TWO OR three days after this his lordship told Yoshihide that he was ready to fulfill his promise. Of course the carriage was not to be burned at Horikawa, but rather at a country house outside the capital, which the common people called Yukige. Though it had formerly been the residence of his lordship's younger sister, no one had occupied Yukige for many years. It had a large garden that had been allowed to run wild. People attributed its neglect to many causes: for instance, they said that on moonless nights the daimyo's dead sister, wearing a strange scarlet skirt, still walked along the corridors without touching the floor. The mansion was desolate enough by day, but at night, with the splashing sounds of the invisible brook and the monstrous shapes of the night herons flying through the starlight, it was entirely eerie.

As it happened, that night was moonless and pitch black. The light of the oil lamps shone on his lordship, clad in pale yellow robes and a dark purple skirt embroidered with crests, sitting on the veranda on a plaited straw cushion with a white silk embroidered hem. I need not add that before and behind, to the left and to the right of him, five or six attendants stood respectfully. The choice of one was significant—he was a powerful samurai who had eaten human flesh to stay his hunger at the Battle of Michinoku, and since then, they say, he had been able to tear apart the horns of a live deer. His long sword sticking out behind like a gull's tail, he stood, a forbidding figure, beneath the veranda. The flickering light of the lamps, now bright, now dark, shone on the scene. So dreadful a horror was on us that we scarcely knew whether we dreamed or waked.

They had drawn the carriage into the garden. There it stood, its heavy roof weighing down the darkness. There were no oxen harnessed to it, and the end of its black tongue rested on a stand. When we saw its gold metalwork glittering like stars, we felt chilly in spite of the spring night. The carriage was heavily closed with blue blinds edged with embroidery, so that we could not know what was inside. Around it stood attendants with torches in their hands, worrying over the smoke that drifted towards the veranda and waiting significantly.

Yoshihide knelt facing the veranda, a little distance off. He seemed smaller and shabbier than usual, the starry sky seemed to oppress him. The man who squatted behind him was doubtless an apprentice. The two of them were at some distance from me and below the veranda so that I could not be sure of the colour of their clothes.

17

IT MUST have been near midnight. The darkness that enveloped the brook seemed to watch our very breathing. In it was only the faint stir of the night wind that carried the sooty smell of the pine torches to us. For some time his lordship watched the scene in silence, motionless. Presently, he moved forward a little and called sharply, "Yoshihide."

The latter must have made some sort of reply, though what I heard sounded more like a groan.

"Yoshihide, tonight in accordance with your request lam going to burn this carriage for you."

His lordship glanced sidelong at those around him and seemed to exchange a meaningful smile with one or two, though I may have only imagined it. Yoshihide raised his head fearfully and looked up at the veranda, but said nothing and did not move from where he squatted.

"Look. That is the carriage I have always used. You recognize it, don't you? I am going to burn it and show you blazing hell itself."

Again his lordship paused and winked at his attendants. Suddenly his tone became unpleasant. "In that carriage, by my command, is a female malefactor. Therefore, when it is fired her flesh will be roasted, her bones burnt, she will die in extreme agony. Never again will you find such a model for the completion of your screen. Do not flinch from looking at snow-white skin inflamed with fire. Look well at her black hair dancing up in sparks."

His lordship ceased speaking for the third time. I don't know what thoughts were in his mind, but his shoulders shook with silent laughter. "Posterity will never see anything like it. I'll watch it from here. Come, come, lift up the blinds and show Yoshihide the woman inside."

At the daimyo's word one of the attendants, holding high his pine torch in one hand, walked up to the carriage without more ado, stretched out his free hand, and raised the blind. The flickering torch burned with a sharp crackling noise. It brightly lit up the narrow interior of the carriage, showing a woman on its couch, cruelly bound with chains. Who was she? Ah, it could not be! She was clad in a gorgeously embroidered cherry-patterned mantle; her black hair, alluringly loosened, hung straight down; the golden hairpins set at different angles gleamed beautifully, but there was a gag over her mouth tied behind her neck. The small slight body, the modest profile—the attire only was different—it was Yuzuki. I nearly cried aloud.

At that moment the samurai opposite me got to his feet hastily and put his hand on his sword. It must have been Yoshihide that he glared at. Startled I glanced at the artist. He seemed half-stunned by what he now saw. Suddenly he leapt up, stretched out both his arms before him, and forgetting everything else, began to run towards the carriage. Unfortunately, as I have already said, he was at some distance in the shadow, and I could not see the expression on his face. But that was momentary, for now I saw that it was absolutely colourless. His whole form cleaving the darkness appeared vividly before our eyes in the half-light—he was held in space, it seemed, by some invisible power that lifted him from the ground. Then, at his lordship's command, "Set fire," the carriage with its passenger, bathed in the light of the torches that were tossed on to it, burst into flames.

18

AS WE watched. the flames enveloped the carriage.
The purple tassels that hung from the roof corners
swung as though in a wind, while from below them
the smoke swirled white against the blackness of the
night. So frightful was it that the bamboo blinds, the
hangings, the metal ornaments in the roof, seemed to
be flying in the leaping shower of sparks. The tongues
of flames that licked up from beneath the blinds, those
serried flames that shot up into the sky, seemed to be
celestial flames of the sun fallen to the earth. I had
almost shouted before, but now I felt completely overwhelmed and dumbfounded; mouth agape, I could do
nothing but watch the dreadful spectacle. But the father—Yoshihide ...

I still remember the expression on his face. He had
started involuntarily toward the carriage, but when the
flame blazed up he stopped, arms outstretched, and
with piercing eyes watched the smoke and fire that enveloped the carriage as though he would be drawn into
it. The blaze lit his wrinkled face so clearly that even
the hairs of his head could be seen distinctly: in the
depths of his wide staring eyes, in his drawn distorted
lips, in his twitching cheeks, the grief, dread, and be-
wilderment that passed through his soul were clearly
inscribed. A robber, guilty of unspeakable crimes and
about to be beheaded, or dragged before the court of
the Ten Kings, could hardly have looked more ago-
nized. Even that gigantic samurai changed colour and
looked fearfully at the Lord of Horikawa.

But the latter, without taking his eyes off the carriage, merely bit his lips or laughed unpleasantly

from time to time. As for the carriage and its passenger, that girl—I am not brave enough to tell you all I saw. Her white face, choking in the smoke, looked upward; her long loosened hair fluttered in the smoke, her cherry-patterned mantle—how beautiful it was! What a terrible spectacle! But when the night wind dropped and the smoke was drawn away to the other side, where gold dust seemed to be scattered above the red flames, when the girl gnawed her gag, writhing so that it seemed the chains must burst, I, and even the gigantic samurai wondered whether we were not spectators of the torments of hell itself, and our flesh crept.

Then once more we thought the night wind stirred in the treetops of the garden. As that sound passed over the sky, something black that neither touched ground nor flew through the sky, dancing like a ball, leaped from the roof of the house into the blazing carriage. Into the crumbling blinds, cinnabar-stained, he fell, and putting his arms around the straining girl, he cried shrill and long into the smoke, a cry that sounded like tearing silk. He repeated it two or three times, then we forgot ourselves and shouted out together. Against the transparent curtain of flames, clinging to the girl's shoulder, was Yoshihide, Yoshihide the monkey, that had been left tied at the mansion.

19

BUT WE saw him only for a moment. Like gold leaf on a brown screen the sparks climbed into the sky. The monkey and Yuzuki were hidden in black smoke while the carriage blazed away with a dreadful noise in the garden. It was a pillar of fire—those awful flames stabbed the very sky.

In front of that pillar Yoshihide stood rooted. Then, wonderful to say, over the wrinkled face of this Yoshihide, who had seemed to suffer on a previous occasion the tortures of hell, over his face the light of an inexpressible ecstasy passed, and forgetful even of his lordship's presence he folded his arms and stood watching. It was almost as if he did not see his daughter dying in agony. Rather he seemed to delight in the beautiful colour of the flames and the form of a woman in torment.

What was most remarkable was not that he was joyfully watching the death of his daughter. It was rather that in him seemed to be a sternness not human, like the wrath of a kingly lion seen in a dream. Surprised by the fire, flocks of night birds that cried and clamoured seemed thicker—though it may have been my imagination—around Yoshihide's cap. Maybe those soulless birds seemed to see a weird glory like a halo around that man's head. If the birds were attracted, how much more were we, the servants, filled with a strange feeling of worship as we watched Yoshihide. We quaked within, we held our breath, we watched him like a Buddha unveiled. The roaring of the fire that filled the air, and Yoshihide, his soul taken captive by it, standing there motionless—what awe we felt, what intense pleasure at this spectacle. Only his lordship sat on the veranda as though he were a different sort of being. He grew pale, foam gathered on his lips, he clutched his purple-skirted knee with both hands, he panted like some thirsty animal …

20

IT GOT around that his lordship had burnt a carriage at Yukige that night—though of course nobody said anything—and a great variety of opinions were expressed. The first and most prevalent rumour was that he had burnt Yoshihide's daughter to death in resentment over thwarted love. But there was no doubt that it was the daimyo's purpose to punish the perversity of the artist, who was painting the Hell Screen, even if he had to kill someone to do so. In fact, his lordship himself told me this.

Then there was much talk about the stony-heartedness of Yoshihide, who saw his daughter die in flames before his eyes and yet wanted to paint the screen. Some called him a beast of prey in human form, rendered incapable of human love by a picture. The Abbot of Yokogawa often said, "A man's genius may be very great, great his art, but only an understanding of the Five Virtues[3] will save him from Hell."

However, about a month later the Hell Screen was completed. Yoshihide immediately took it to the mansion and showed it with great deference to the Lord of Horikawa. The Abbot happened to be visiting his lordship at the time, and when he looked at it he must have been properly startled by the storm of fire that rages across the firmament on one of the leaves. He pulled a wry face, stared hard at Yoshihide, but said, "Well done," in spite of himself. I still remember the forced laugh with which his lordship greeted this.

From that time on, there was none that spoke badly of Yoshihide, at least in the mansion. And anyone who saw the screen, even if he hated the artist before, was struck solemn, because he felt that he was experiencing Hell's most exquisite tortures.

But by that time Yoshihide was no longer among the living. The night after the screen was finished he hanged himself from a beam in his studio. With his only daughter preceding him he felt, no doubt, that he could not bear to live on in idleness. His remains still lie within the ruins of his house. The rains and winds of many decades have bleached the little stone that marked his grave, and the moss has covered it in oblivion.

Notes

1 The third of the Five Great Kings, guarding the center. In his right hand he holds a sword to strike the demons, in his left, a cord to bind them.

2 Judges of the underworld.

3 The Five Virtues of Confucius: Humanity, Justice, Propriety, Wisdom and Fidelity.

The Spider's Thread

BUDDHA WAS STROLLING ALONE AROUND THE LOTUS pond in Paradise. In the pond the pearly white lotus blossoms were wafting out from their centres an indescribably sweet fragrance. It was morning in Paradise.

Presently Buddha paused on the edge of the pond, and looking down into it between the lotus leaves which covered the water, watched what was going on below. Since the lotus pond was directly over the Pit of Hell, the river Styx and the Mount of Needles were as clearly visible through the crystal clear water as in a peep-show.

As Buddha watched, his eyes lit on a man called Kandata writhing in the bottom of Hell with all the other sinners. Now Kandata had been a notorious robber who had murdered, set fires and perpetrated various evil deeds. However it was recorded that he had done just one good deed. One day as he was going through a deep forest he happened to see a little spider crawling along the path. He lifted his foot and was about to crush it when he stopped. "No, no, this is a little creature but it has life, and it would be a pity to take its life." Suddenly he changed his mind and spared the spider's life. As he gazed down on the landscape of Hell, Buddha remembered how Kandata had saved the spider's life, as a reward for just this one good deed he decided to get Kandata out of Hell if possible. As he looked around, on a jade-green lotus leaf Buddha saw a heavenly spider spinning his beautiful silvery thread. Gently he picked up the spider's thread and lowered it straight down between the pearly white lotus flowers to the depths of Hell.

2

HERE IS the Pit of Hell Kandata was floating and sinking in the Lake of Blood. Down here it was pitch black wherever you looked; if there were faint gleams it was only the needles on the fearsome Mount of Needles. All was hopeless. It was almost as silent as the grave; all that could be heard were the sighs of the sinners. That was because they were so exhausted by the Tortures of Hell that they did not have the strength to cry out. And that notorious robber Kandata, choking in the blood of the Lake of Blood could only flounder around like a dying frog.

At this point Kandata happened by chance to raise his head and look at the sky above the Lake of Blood. And there in the silent darkness from the distant, oh so distant sky came dropping down over his head a silvery spider's thread, so slender and so silent it seemed to fear being seen. When Kandata saw it, he involuntarily clapped his hands and rejoiced. If he could cling to this thread and climb up as far as it went he would certainly be able to get out of Hell. He would be able to get out of the Lake of Blood, he could get up over the

Mount of Needles, if lucky he might even be able to get up to Paradise.

As soon as the thought came to him Kandata clutched the spider's thread with both hands and started climbing up hand over hand. Since he had been a great robber, of course he had practiced this sort of thing from of old.

However there is a great distance between Paradise and Hell; miles upon countless miles separate them. No matter how hard he worked, he could not easily climb all the way up. He had not gone far when he became tired. It couldn't be helped, he had to rest. As he had succeeded in climbing up quite a distance, the Lake of Blood was now hidden in darkness. The dreadful Mount of Needles, gleaming faintly was miles away below his feet. If he went on climbing at this rate, he might get out of Hell more easily than he thought. Clinging to the spider's thread with both hands in a voice that had not shouted for years, he laughed and bellowed "I've done it, I've done it." But then he noticed that following him up the thread, like a procession of ants, climbed the sinners. When he saw this, his big mouth agape like a fool, in astonishment and fear his eyes blinked busily. Could this slender spider's thread, which might have broken with only his weight, carry all those mortals. If perchance this thread broke now would not also he, who had got up this far, fall headlong back into Hell? That would be terrible. While he was thinking this, the sinners by the hundreds of thousands kept swarming up from the Lake of Blood along the slender thread in single file. Something had to be done. The thread might break at any moment and there was no doubt about it, down he would fall.

Thereupon Kandata bellowed. "Hey, you sinners. This is my spider's thread. Who allowed you to climb it? Get off. Get off." At that very instant, the spider's thread that had bravely borne Kandata went PING and broke. Kandata was helpless. In a twinkling, like a top cutting the wind, he fell head over heels down into the Depths of Hell.

And the thread of the heavenly spider, hung shining thin in the moonless, starless sky.

3

BUDDHA STANDING on the edge of the lotus pond of Paradise watched it all patiently from beginning to end, and when Kandata fell like a stone to the bottom of the Lake of Blood, he again began his stroll with a sad look on his countenance. Kandata, who wanted to save only himself, had received the punishment for his merciless heart. It was the meanness of the robber, thought Buddha. The lotus flowers of the pond cared nothing. Their calyxes swayed to and fro and sent out ceaselessly from the pistils in their centre, their indescribably sweet fragrance. It was about noon in Paradise.